First published in Great Britain by Scribo MMXI,
Scribo, a division of Book House, an imprint of
The Salariya Book Company
25 Marlborough Place, Brighton, BN1 1UB
www.salariya.com

Book Design by David Salariya

Printed and bound in Dubai

The text for this book is set in Cochin
The display types are set in Nikona X1

www.scribobooks.com

CHRONOSPHERE

Book 2

Malfunction

Alex Woolf

Scribo
A division of Book House

CONTENTS

The Chronosphere is a world liberated from the clock – a place in which time moves as fast or as slowly as we collectively desire. We who dwell in this world have no need of timetables or schedules. We have stripped time of its qualities of transience and motion and imbued it with the stillness and tranquility of space. We are revolutionaries, overthrowing the tyranny of hours, minutes and seconds; we are pioneers, colonising rich and fertile new temporal pastures; we are chrononauts, venturing into that vast, uncharted territory that lies between each tick of the clock, each blink of the eye and each beat of the heart.

Chronomaster Edo Carinae

PROLOGUE

y the late 22nd century, time had become a commodity that could be bought and sold, just like goods and property. Shortly after his 18th birthday Raffi Delgado went to the Time Store and bought himself a year. He was shown into the Chronosphere – a place where time moved half a million times slower than in the real world. Raffi's year in the Chronosphere would take up just one minute of Earth time.

The Chronosphere at first seemed like paradise. Raffi was given his own domicile in Time Tower, the vast hourglass-shaped residential block that stood at the centre of the Chronosphere. He met a group of friends and they enjoyed an almost perfect, pleasure-filled existence. Yet Raffi sensed that all was not completely right with the 'Sphere'. For one thing, teenagers kept disappearing. Then there were his odd, disturbing visions of two of his friends – Lastara Blue and Jonah Grey – looking very old indeed. He was also unnerved by the sinister Secrocon Police, who could literally 'arrest'

people by dilating them to normal time, causing them to freeze.

When his friend Dario was arrested, Raffi tried to visit him, but instead found himself joining Dario in the Re-Education Centre, a brutal subterranean gulag where teenage prisoners were unhitched from the normal flow of time and placed in 'time-locked' cells. One girl he met there had been time-reversed and was living her life backwards. With the help of a former inmate, Septimus Watts, Raffi and Dario managed to escape back to the 'Topside' by changing their identities. Dario was now called Christo Ellis; Raffi's new name was Michael Storm. The boys were given CID (Cognitive Inference Deception) disguises. These were special masks composed of light that worked in the manner of an optical illusion to fool observers into seeing only what they expect to see: an anonymous human face. In this way, Raffi and Dario were able to continue their lives on the Topside without being discovered.

But Raffi's new identity did cause some tensions with Brigitte, his emotionally unstable MAID (one of the artificially intelligent computers that came with each domicile). Brigitte had enjoyed romantic relations with the original Michael Storm and now demanded the same from Raffi – if he didn't want her to inform the authorities of her suspicions that he was an imposter. Raffi was forced to oblige, and each evening he entered the virtuarium, a virtual reality environment in which MAIDs can take on human form and interact in human ways with their masters. But when she offered to alter her look to make herself more pleasing to him, Raffi turned her into an almost exact copy of Anna, the beautiful, time-reversed girl he'd encountered on the Underside.

As if being blackmailed by his own MAID wasn't enough, Raffi's social circle suddenly lost half its diameter when he parted ways with two of his four friends – Lastara and Jonah. Lastara was a paradisiac-popping part-time model and full-time hedonist. Raffi had always had his doubts about her. She treated her boyfriend, Dario Brice, shabbily, and her long-term admirer, Jonah, even worse. When Dario was arrested, Lastara took up with Raffi's hoverbiking arch rival, the part-cyborg Red Oakes. But what really decided the issue for Raffi was his discovery that Lastara had been paying for her expensive lifestyle by secretly working for Secrocon, the mysterious organisation that ran the Sphere. Lastara had been kidnapping teenagers and sending them to the Underside for who-knew-what purpose. Jonah, despite learning of Lastara's extra-curricular activities, couldn't bring himself to abandon her. Perhaps Raffi shouldn't have been surprised by this – after all, Jonah had chosen to continue living in the Sphere, even though it was making him sick, just so he could remain close to her. Despising Lastara for her wickedness, and Jonah for his weakness, Raffi ceased virtually all contact with both of them.

But he still had a firm friendship with Dario and a slightly more ambiguous one with Sal. Dario was a handsome, sporty, big-hearted fellow, disposed to think well of everyone, especially Sal, who he had been in love with for a long time. As far as Raffi was concerned, Sal was actually a good foil for the relentlessly cheerful Dario. Quiet-spoken, hard-edged and cynical – easily overlooked in a crowd, despite her bright blue hair – Sal's only purpose in entering the Chronosphere was to find her long-lost sister, Anna, who she believed had been kidnapped and taken there by a man called Avon Drak. Raffi suspected Anna was the time-reversed girl he'd met during his spell on the Underside, but he didn't dare say this to Sal as the last thing he wanted was to get caught up in a rescue mission and have Secrocon after him again. All he wanted, in fact, was to relax and have a good time.

And now, with just four months to go before the end of his year, he seemed to have finally got his wish. Brigitte was behaving herself – more or less – and Raffi's days had fallen into a pleasant routine of hoverbike racing, wave riding and air tennis, while his evenings were spent at the holoplex or in his domicile watching sensovision. All very pleasant and yet…

CHAPTER ONE

⏳

THE MALFUNCTION

…ever so slightly dull. What use was all this time if every day was the same? Even the appeal of hanging out with Dario and Sal was beginning to pall when conversations, unspiced by sufficient news, became circular and repetitive. A loner at heart, Raffi found himself spending increasing amounts of time keeping his own company. As a result he became more observant and – perhaps before most other people – began to notice changes in the Chronosphere. Some of these changes were obvious to him, others less so.

The days, for one thing, were definitely growing warmer, and he noticed that fewer people were choosing to mill around in the public squares and shopping malls. The parks and gardens, designed as spaces where people could linger and saunter or just stand and stare, were no longer attracting the people-watchers and attention-seekers, the gamesplayers and spectators; they were no longer meeting points for friends and lovers, but simply anonymous spaces that had to be crossed to get from A to B. Many were choosing to stay in air-conditioned buildings rather than face the heat of the day. Others were simply leaving. Every day, he stood on the balcony overlooking the terminus platform and watched transradials filled with people moving out towards the temp-al chambers at the rim of the Sphere, and returning virtually empty.

And there were subtle changes in those who remained. In the atria and shopping malls, people were less inclined to stop and chat. There were fewer smiles, less laughter. And the laughter there was sounded forced, like the barking of anxious dogs, like laughter between strangers. It's not just me and Jonah, thought Raffi, it's everyone. We're becoming strangers to each other.

Raffi didn't mention any of this to Dario, and Dario said nothing to him – in fact, he remained as bluff and hearty as ever, as if nothing had changed at all. Sal, however, didn't hesitate to complain about the heat or reflect on how empty the Sphere was becoming. Her latest theory was that the Chronosphere was getting warmer because the speed of time was slowing. According to Sal, it might eventually dwindle to a complete standstill and they'd be cut permanently adrift from the real world. 'We'll become the Dome that Time Forgot,' she warned.

Other odd things started happening. Raffi would order a meal from Brigitte and would get something entirely different. The bread he ordered sometimes tasted less than fresh. Once he was served the same meal on three consecutive days. At first he thought this was just Brigitte playing her little games and he didn't report it to anyone. But then Dario mentioned that his meal service was becoming erratic. Soon Raffi was overhearing similar stories from his neighbours on Floor 150.

Again, people tended to talk about this as just one of those things: a blip in the normal levels of service, soon to be put right. They could almost have been quoting the standard response from Secrocon Complaints Department. Sal was the only person Raffi knew of to speculate that things might be more serious: perhaps a major breakdown in the food supply. Why else did there appear to be a surfeit of certain foods, while others had disappeared from the menu? But Raffi, like most people, tended to believe the authorities when they reported, via the MAIDs, that the situation was 'in hand', 'under control', 'routine'. 'Continue as normal' they advised, and Raffi was happy to do just that.

And so the people who chose, for one reason or another, to remain in the Chronosphere – and there were several thousand of them – found ways of adapting to the new conditions. The outside places – the parks, meadows, streets and squares – became sweltering, semi-abandoned deserts during the day, while human life congregated in the air-conditioned interiors: the atria, domiciles, sports centres, holoplexes and covered arcades. Only in the cooler evenings did chrono-folk venture outside. And when the sameness of the food supplied to the domiciles became less than tolerable, people gravitated to the eathouses and bars and tried to ignore the fact that the menus were gradually shrinking and the choices becoming limited even in the classiest eateries. The situation was, as Sal warned, unsustainable. But Raffi, like almost everyone else, preferred to follow the advice they were given and 'continue as normal'. And every day, the transradials took more people to the perimeter and returned empty.

Who could say how long the situation might have remained like this, and how long the 10,000 or so die-hards might have clung on? Quite a while, Raffi had to assume. For Lastara Blue was certainly not the only one to be blinded by her addiction to the Chronosphere's promise of endless pleasure – there were many others like her. No one can know what would have happened, because events were soon to take a different course. Or, to be precise, one specific event was about to occur that would change absolutely everything.

⧗

The event, which later came to be known as the Malfunction, took place at some point towards the middle of Week 43 of Chronospheric Year 122 – in other words, around the end of Raffi's ninth month in the Sphere. Afterwards there was some disagreement as to exactly when it took place. This was partly because the subsequent period was so confused and frightening that people's thoughts were focused on survival rather than keeping accurate records for posterity. Also, the Malfunction itself happened in such a quiet and unassuming way that it was not at first recognised as anything very significant, even by those who witnessed it, and it would be a few days before the majority woke up to the fact that something momentous had happened. A stubborn minority, including Lastara Blue, continued long after that time to maintain that the Malfunction signified nothing of importance whatsoever.

Raffi had an inkling that something was up sooner than most because of his habit of frequenting the Time Tower Terminus and watching the transradials arriving and departing. On the morning in question, he was at his usual spot on the balcony overlooking the platform when he spotted something unusual. For the first time in many weeks, a transradial had arrived from the perimeter full to bursting with people. Hello! thought Raffi. Perhaps things are finally looking up. A fresh injection of new blood: that's what this place needs. But then he looked more closely at the people disembarking and noticed the slumped shoulders, the furrowed brows, the anxious conversations. These didn't look like new arrivals. No, these were people who had been hoping to leave but were now back here, and not happy about it. Ten minutes later, another transradial arrived from a different part of the perimeter, carrying a cargo of similarly thwarted passengers. Intrigued, Raffi remained at his post until lunchtime. In all, six transradials returned from the rim, all full of unhappy would-be departees. He descended the spiral glass conveyor to the platform and asked an android guard what was going on. 'Problem with the temp-al chambers,' he was told. 'I'm sure they'll have it fixed by this afternoon.'

The problem wasn't fixed that afternoon, nor the following day. By Day 3, rim-bound transradials were being cancelled. There were angry scenes at the Terminus. Passengers simply refused to believe that all the temp-al chambers could malfunction at precisely the same moment. What about the service temp-al ducts – the ones used to send in supplies? Couldn't they use those? The android guards were not programmed to deal with this level of outrage, and a flustered stationmaster emerged from his office. 'The problem is an external one,' he announced to the crowd of angry patrons. 'There's nothing we can do about it from this side. But don't worry. Urgent communications are being made to the outside world. I'm sure we'll have those temp-al chambers functioning again in no time.'

Raffi, listening in on the edge of the crowd, was doubtful about this. Even if the fault was relatively easy to put right, the time differential between the outside world and the Sphere was so huge that it could be three or four years at the very least before the temp-al chambers were fixed. The thought scared him. What if the food ran out? What if…? He extinguished the thought – he was becoming adept at that. Just focus on the next event, he told himself – and he thought about his holoflick plans that evening. Soon enough, he felt calm again.

By the end of Day 3, the malfunction remained stubbornly unresolved. Yet it was still only a malfunction with a small 'm'. It would not acquire the status of the Malfunction, with definite article and big 'M', until Day 5. News of the problem took a while to spread beyond the immediate confines of the terminus. There was no mention of it in the Tower Times, as always fulfilling its journalistic brief to report nothing of significance whatsoever. And the Time Tower grapevine, which had once been such a key disseminator of news and gossip, had withered in recent weeks, thanks to the mass departures and accompanying decline in community spirit. As Raffi had noted, people had become strangers to each other, and consequently the natural osmosis by which information filters through a group now failed to occur. The frustrated passengers remained defiantly encamped on the station platform, or else returned to their domiciles to fume in private.

In fact, Raffi may have been one of the first to spread word of the problem beyond the Terminus building when he met up with Dario and Sal at the holoplex on Season Square on the evening of Day 3. He would always remember the look Sal gave him when he casually mentioned it to them. Her face turned grey and rigid, almost like stone. Her hand was like ice on his wrist. 'This is it,' she said quietly. Then Dario cut in with something upbeat like: 'Oh, they'll get it fixed soon enough. The Sphere is crawling with engineers and technicians.'

Raffi was back at his post on the morning of Day 4 – his balcony seat at the theatre of the unfolding crisis, which had become more absorbing to him than anything else in his current life. There was more confrontation and anger on the platform, which was by now a lot more crowded. But people had yet to learn the art of coordinated protest. The habit of individualism had burrowed too deep. The most vociferous would remonstrate with the station staff and point their fingers at the sky and make more angry calls on their wearables, while others would just stare pathetically at the monorail, hoping that a rim-bound transradial would miraculously appear.

By around midday, news had at last begun to ripple outwards from the terminus, and the curious began to descend from the lower atrium to join Raffi at the balcony. There was little talk amongst them, strangers all. But one or two broke the habit and asked Raffi what was up. When he told them, there was general surprise, but not much alarm. Most were certain it would be fixed soon enough. So far, everyone saw it as a problem affecting only those who wished to leave. It would be some hours before the realisation dawned that the service temp-al ducts were also failing to operate, preventing supplies from getting in.

At around 3 o'clock, a fight broke out on the platform between two would-be passengers. Raffi hadn't witnessed the beginning, but understood quickly that it was a territorial issue. By this time, the passengers had staked out areas of the platform for themselves and their luggage, with the prime positions nearest the platform edge going to those who had been there the longest – the Day 1-ers as they called themselves. It seemed that a Day 2-er, or perhaps even an upstart Day 3-er, had tried to muscle in on one of these prime sites, triggering the conflict. In such a crowded space, it was inevitable that a tussle like this would spread, and it wasn't long before half a dozen were throwing punches, elbowing ribs and kicking suitcases. The balcony crowd were quietly thrilled by this spectacle and began taking bets on the outcome. One man was sent tumbling off the platform to end up draped over the monorail with his heels in the concrete well. Fortunately for him the powerful superconducting magnets had been switched off. Secrocon police swooped suddenly into view on big blue hoverbikes, appealing for calm on their loudhailers. The sight of them quickly brought order the crowd, and the shouts and cries subsided to disgruntled murmurs. What interested Raffi was how mature and smartly turned out the aggressors had been. These weren't scruffy teenagers engaged in a brawl, but business types in suits and ties defending their territory like cavemen.

An irate voice in the crowd behind him caught his attention. A woman was speaking into her wearable. 'What do you mean you can't deliver it? It was scheduled to arrive today. Don't you understand, it contains important medications for my husband. It's a priority package.' She switched off the wearable in a huff. 'Now they're saying the service temp-al ducts aren't functioning either. And my husband needs his medication today!' The wider implications of this news didn't occur to the woman, preoccupied as she was with her immediate needs, but a kind of collective nervous tic ran through the crowd as her words registered.

'Oh dear, whatever next!' shrilled one lady. But no one dared say more.

CHAPTER TWO

SUBWAY INCIDENT

In these disturbing times the cooler evening hours could offer chrononauts a faint reminder of how things used to be. One could no longer say that the boulevards bustled or that the cafés thronged, but small groups did still venture out, keeping at least some of the al fresco caterers and retailers financially afloat and giving nostalgic pause to the watchers from the Time Tower balconies. It was Raffi's custom to spend the evenings on Dario's 120th-floor balcony, sipping cider coolfizz and watching the scenes below. On the evening of the fourth day after the Malfunction, however, there was virtually no one to be seen in the streets or parks, and not a single airborne hoverbike. Many of the neighbouring domicile windows were shuttered. An odd hush and stillness had descended, as people retreated to their private sanctuaries.

At 21.00 hours there came official acknowledgement, at last, that something had happened. In every domicile, the MAIDs broadcast the same words at the same time – only their individually customised voices differed. Raffi and Dario listened to Mandy, Christo's MAID, confirm that both the temp-al chambers and service temp-al ducts were currently out of action. They were reassured that engineers were working around the clock to try to remedy the situation, although the fault appeared to be an external one. A message was in the process of being sent to the outside world – because of differences in temporal velocity, messages had to be sent very gradually, over a period of days, in order to be intelligible to outside listeners. Confirmation that this message had been received and understood was expected in about two to three weeks, and assuming internal engineers were unsuccessful, external staff would almost certainly have the temp-al chambers back in working order within a year. Raffi and Dario could almost hear the Tower-wide groan that greeted this last prognosis – although Raffi, for one, almost felt relieved. A year, if anything, sounded optimistic.

'In the meantime,' the message continued, 'we have plentiful supplies of food and drink and sufficient energy in reserve to keep us going for several years, if necessary, so there is absolutely no need to panic, and customers are advised to continue as normal. However, we do advise customers not to be wasteful in their habits. Supplies may be plentiful at the moment, but they can quickly run low if consumed irresponsibly. Most importantly, customers should not try to force their way out of the Chronosphere. The consequences of such an act could be disastrous for everyone. For customers' safety, we are stationing police chrono-sans at all reception points and service exits, and we are placing electrified fencing around the entire perimeter of the Chronosphere. Please remember, we are doing this for your safety and security. We advise everyone once again to stay calm and continue as normal.'

'Jeebus,' breathed Dario, when the broadcast was over. 'A whole year!'

'At the very least, I would say,' said Raffi.

Dario poured Raffi some more cider coolfizz. 'What was all that about not trying to force our way out? Why would it be dangerous for everyone?'

Raffi shrugged. 'Jonah would know.'

'Shall we call him?'

'Haven't spoken to him in weeks.'

Dario called Jonah. 'Hey mate! How the hooly are you?'

Raffi stared at his hands as he listened to Dario's side of the conversation. It would be good to see Jonah again.

'Come on up here on your bike,' Dario was saying. 'Michael and me are on the balcony at mine. We want to hear your thoughts on all this.'

Raffi stiffened. He nudged Dario, who added with a smile: 'And don't bring you-know-who.'

'You didn't have to put it like that,' Raffi groaned.

But Dario only laughed: 'It's okay. He understands.'

Jonah looked sleepy and pasty-faced as he docked. 'I hope they fix this thing soon,' he said, removing his helmet. 'I'm expecting a delivery of medications in a few weeks.'

Raffi looked at him, concerned. 'It may take a lot longer than that.'

Jonah only shrugged tiredly. There was no embrace for Raffi or Dario this time. He simply slumped into a chair and accepted Dario's offer of a drink.

'So what's so bad about trying to punch a hole in the Sphere wall?' asked Dario. 'If things got bad, we could escape that way, couldn't we?'

Jonah shook his head. 'For one thing, the wall's a lot thicker than you might think. It would take a hell of a lot of explosive power. And for another, it would quite likely kill everyone in here.'

'How so?'

'Think of the pressurised cabin of a jet aircraft. Air

pressure is increased at high altitudes to counteract the low atmospheric pressure outside. Okay?'

'Okay.'

'Well, the Chronosphere is based on the same principle, except it's not air that's been pressurised in here, but time. Now what happens if you fire a gun through the window of a pressurised cabin of a jet?''

'Rapid depressurisation,' said Raffi. 'People get sucked out.'

'Exactly. And the same thing would happen here, only with time rather than with air. Time would rush out of here, like air out of a burst balloon.'

'And what would that feel like?'

'Well, no one knows for sure, but anyone caught in its blast would probably age horribly in a matter of seconds and become withered, shrunken old husks of skin and bone!' Jonah grinned, almost as though he relished the prospect. 'It's the Moon Effect, of course.'

The Moon Effect was something Jonah had often talked of before, though Raffi had never heard any official confirmation that it existed, and Lastara, for one, dismissed it as a complete myth. As Raffi understood it, a kind of tension or imbalance existed in the Chronosphere because the people and objects within it occupied time more densely than they occupied space. Jonah described it as a 'kink in space-time'. This Moon Effect, according to Jonah's speculations, grew stronger the longer one remained inside the Chronosphere, and it wasn't entirely harmless. Jonah believed it explained his illness and Lastara's extreme behaviour.

⧗

The following day – the fifth since the Malfunction – Raffi returned to his vigil on the balcony. The station platform was now virtually empty. Only a few diehard Day-1ers remained, mad-eyed and unshaven, jealously guarding territories that no one was any longer interested in stealing from them. Most passengers had by now accepted that there would be no transradials for the forseeable future and had returned to their domiciles. With no action at the terminus, Raffi decided to take a hike over to the tenniplex on Interim and Sixth to see if he could get a game with someone. As the glass doors that led onto the concourse swished open, he was almost knocked back by the heat. It was worse than he'd ever experienced. He quickly retreated inside the building, then descended to the terminus. He could have taken one of the internal transradials to his destination, but he preferred to navigate a route through the spidery network of pedestrian subways that crisscrossed the Sphere just below ground level. These were, at least, cool, if dull and airless. Quite a number of people had made the same choice, and the going was slow. A tall, disshevelled man in front of Raffi was pushing at the backs of the slower people in front of him, urging them to go faster. 'Come on, come on,' he shouted. 'Haven't got all day!'

A man in front stopped and turned on him. 'Hey, watch who you're pushing, mister!' and he shoved the tall man in the chest.

The tall man swore and pulled out a large knife. It looked like a standard kitchen knife taken from one of the domiciles. The people immediately around him gasped and tried to get out of the way. He jabbed at the shorter man. It looked to Raffi like a little jab, a warning, nothing more. But then he saw blood flowering on the man's white t-shirt and watched him sink to his knees. The crowd began to surge forwards, and Raffi was carried helplessly along with them. He felt nauseous from the sight of the blood and the smell of panic around him.

CHAPTER THREE

⧗

LASTARA'S STORY

fter that experience, Raffi couldn't face the prospect of tennis, so he slunk back to his domicile.

'Hello Michael,' said Brigitte. 'You're not usually here at this time of day.'

'I have a headache,' he told her. 'Can you dim the windows, please?'

'As you wish,' she said. 'Of course you realise that window dimming won't be necessary as of tomorrow.'

'Oh, why's that?

'As an energy-saving measure, Secrocon have decided to limit the amount of daylight in the Sphere to just two hours per day. That will also help to lower the temperature.'

'So we're going to become a nocturnal society,' he said. 'Did they put this to the vote, or did they just decide among themselves?'

'It's clearly in everyone's best interests,' said Brigitte, sidestepping the question.

'Clearly,' he agreed, before falling into a doze.

⧗

An hour or so later, he was awoken by Brigitte. 'There's a young lady here to see you. She says she's an old friend. I've shown her into the lounge.'

'Is it Sal?'

'No. The name she gave was Lastara Blue.'

This woke him up. 'Lastara, what in hooly is she doing here?'

'She didn't say. Would you like me to power down again?'

'No, and you can turn off those jealousy sensors, B. I feel nothing but intense loathing for this particular person.'

Raffi put his dressing gown on and walked barefoot into the lounge. Lastara sat facing him on the swivel armchair. She smiled when he came in, her pearly front teeth just visible above the luxuriant swell of her lower lip. Her long slim legs were crossed, and visible as far as mid-thigh, thanks to a short skirt. A sober dark jacket partly obscured her close-fitting shiny pale top, and her blonde locks fell neatly in a fan around the top of her shoulders. Despite the skirt, the overall effect was one of businesslike seriousness. She didn't move, but simply locked him in place with her liquid-blue eyes.

'Hello Michael.' Her voice sounded breathy, as though she was subconsciously mimicking Brigitte. 'I hope you don't mind me coming here.'

Raffi scratched his bird's nest of a hairstyle, feeling like a subway tramp compared to this vision of loveliness.

'I know who you are,' she continued recklessly. 'Jonah told me.'

Raffi suppressed an urge to kick her. How could she be so stupid, talking like this in front of Brigitte. Although Brigitte knew the truth about who he was, it was a truth she and he never dared mention. To mention it would force her to act on it, ending their relationship and prompting some tricky questions, such as why she hadn't reported him earlier. She was now as much a party to the deception as he was. And in this game of mutually assured destruction, Lastara's finger was poised playfully on the nuclear trigger. Oh, Jonah was a fool ever to tell her.

'I don't know what you're talking about,' he replied warily.

'No, of course not,' she chuckled, not-very-subtly winking at him. 'But don't worry, darling. I'm not here to talk about you.' Raffi sighed and swallowed with relief. 'I'm here to talk about us.'

'What us?' he asked. 'There is no "us" as far as I'm aware.'

She pursed her lips. 'I know you don't like me. And I can understand why.'

'Why are you here?' he finally asked.

'I'm here because I want to be friends with you. I don't believe we ever gave ourselves a chance. I don't believe you ever gave me a chance.'

He recalled their kiss on his first night in the Sphere. It had been a beautiful kiss – until…

'I believe I gave you every chance, Lastara,' he said. 'Like every man you've ever met, I couldn't see beyond your looks, your charm.'

…until that hideous vision of her as a dessicated corpse had irretrievably wrecked her in his eyes.

He sat down in an upright chair at a safe distance from her, keeping his knees firmly together and his dressing gown fully wrapped. 'But that day when Dario was arrested, and you were only worried about the effect it would have on your career. And your treatment of Jonah, whose health you could have restored any time you wanted by simply taking him out of the Sphere. Not to mention what you did on Calendar Square and no doubt lots of other places, too.' He was referring here to the kidnappings. 'Taking all that into account, you can understand how my attitude towards you might have changed.'

Lastara closed her eyes through most of this, as though it was a litany of charges she had heard all too often before. Then she opened them again. 'My father was killed when I was 16,' she said simply.

Raffi's mouth dropped open. 'I–I'm sorry to hear that,' he stammered. 'But what has that got to do with… I mean how does that excuse the way you treat the people who love you, not to mention innocent strangers.'

'Brutally murdered,' she added, 'right in front of me.' She spoke this coolly, without visible emotion. Her face was a mask.

'Who did this?'

She shook her head. 'I only mention it because…' She lowered her eyes. 'Well, I wish you'd known me before it happened. I think you might have liked me better then.'

'Maybe,' said Raffi.

'No, in fact, I'm sure you would have thought me stupid. I was a hopeless idealist even then. But for that I have to blame my father. I love him and miss him with all my heart – not a day goes by when I don't think about him. But I have to accept that he, at least partly, made me what I am.' She uncrossed her legs and placed her knees together, clasping them with her hands, and for a second Raffi glimpsed her as a little girl. 'He was much more than a father to me,' she smiled, eyes now blurring with memories. 'He was the centre of my world. I didn't have a mum or any siblings, but he made up for that. He filled my early years with wonderful stories and imaginary games. He didn't like talking much about the real world – the world beyond the outland settlement where we lived. And when he finally got around to talking about it, he coated it in sugar and fairy dust and made it seem like a magical kingdom where I could be anything I wanted: an animal doctor, a toymaker or an ice-skating queen. In my father's world, good people were always rewarded and bad people were always punished. When I asked about my mum, he would only say that she was the most beautiful woman who ever lived; she was so beautiful that the gods decided she didn't belong here on earth, so they took her back to paradise. I found out years later that she'd also been killed – blown to bits by a bomb. There wasn't enough of her left to bury... I loved my father, and I love him still, for trying to protect me, but now I wish that he hadn't, or that someone else had been around to give me a different viewpoint. I might have taken steps to protect us better – better than he had anyway. Or, if that wasn't possible, at least I might have been more prepared for what happened next: the break-in and the murder. But then again, what can ever prepare you for something like that: the violent, brutal extermination of every belief, every fantasy, every romantic notion you have about the world. When they killed my father, they left me with nothing, those men. I was a planet without a star, a beach without an ocean, a book without words. I had no sense of location or even self. I was just an empty space where a happy girl had once been. What you see before you now, Michael, is a salvage job. The original Lastara died a long time ago.'

Raffi, still affected by the knife attack he'd witnessed earlier, struggled to process all of this, or think of a suitable response. 'I'm sorry,' he said finally. He shook his head. 'Why do you think they killed him?'

'I'll never know for sure. But I think they were the same people who killed my mother. Perhaps they'd witnessed something they shouldn't have, or perhaps they'd simply done something to upset these people.'

'Don't you want to find out?'

'Once I did, but then I got frightened. I didn't want to end up dead like my parents. Then I met someone who said he could protect me. His name was Ladro di Gioielli.'

'Otherwise known as Avon Drak,' said Raffi, who had met the man during his time on the Underside. Drak was also the man Sal suspected of kidnapping her sister.

Lastara looked up. 'How did you know?'

Raffi was about to relate Sal's story, but then remembered that she'd sworn him to secrecy. 'I met him on the Underside,' he said simply. 'In the Re-Education Centre.'

'Right… Well, he was the one who invited me to enter the Chronosphere. He's been very good to me. I feel safe here. But I'll never be… normal. You know.'

Raffi nodded.

'I didn't want to burden you with all that,' said Lastara, now back to her former, poised self. 'But I had to try and show you that I'm not a complete monster, or rather that I wasn't always a monster. I know I was a bitch about Dario, but he never really cared for me either. He was besotted with Sal, which didn't make me feel great, though I put up with it with reasonable grace. As for Jonah, I love him and he knows I do. We go back such a long way together.'

'If you really loved him, you could have left the Sphere ages ago and allowed him to regain his health.'

'I couldn't do that. It's not something I can ever explain. But Jonah knows the reason.'

'Is it because this place is the magic kingdom your father used to tell you about? In here you can pretend that the world really is covered in sugar and fairydust, just like he said.'

'You can be cruel, you know that.'

'It goes with the territory,' he replied tautly. 'You want to be friends with me, you'll have to put up with my bluntness.'

'I do,' she said meekly, her face obscure in the shadow of her schoolgirl fringe. 'And I will. Do you want to be friends with me?' Her hands wrestled with each other in her lap.

'I feel sorry, really sorry, for what you've had to go through,' sighed Raffi. 'But you can't be friends with someone out of pity.

Besides, you've asked for so much to be taken on trust: you tell me Jonah understands, but I don't know if he really does. And nothing you've said can make me excuse what I saw you do on Calendar Square.'

'It was Jonah who encouraged me to come here today,' she replied. 'He wants us to be friends. If that doesn't convince you that he's cool about all this, I don't know what will. You paint us as though I'm the one with all the power and he's the helpless victim. It's more complex than that. We're both victims; we're both dependent on each other.'

Raffi scratched his head. 'Well that's not the way it looks from here. Anyway, what about the Calendar Square thing? You keep avoiding talking about that.'

'I'm not kidnapping anyone – you got that wrong. I'm sending them to a better place. You don't understand because you've never seen it. But it's a better place, I promise you.'

'I *have* seen it, Lastara, and it's not a better place. It's a torture chamber where kids are taunted with delicious food they can never eat or forced to live their lives backwards or shifted in time so they can't communicate and are forced to live in isolation. It's not a better place.'

'You don't know the full picture, Michael. You jump to conclusions, that's something I know you always like to do. But there's more to it and it's wonderful… Trust me on this.'

'I can't trust you, Lastara. And I can't be your friend, even if I wanted to, because your boyfriend hates me and would like nothing better than to destroy me.'

'You don't have to worry about Red. It's over between us.'

'Even so, I can't be your friend. Not if you can't see that what you did on Calendar Square was wrong.'

'You don't have to worry about Calendar Square,' she said quickly. 'It won't happen again. That phase of the project is over. We're entering a new phase now. There won't be any more "disappearances". I can promise you that.'

'Project? What are you talking about? What project?'

'I can't tell you.' She bit her lip. 'I've given away too much already. I'll only say this: in the new phase we're heading into, you'll have a better chance of survival if we're friends. If you insist on hating and distrusting me, I won't be able to help you – and I can't vouch for your survival.'

She held her hand out to him. 'Friends?'

Raffi shook his head. He had no idea what she'd meant by those vague threats, and he refused to be intimidated by them. 'I can't be your friend, Lastara, but...' But there was Jonah to consider, and the gang that he had once so enjoyed being part of. 'But for Jonah's sake, I'll... be normal with you. We can hang out, if you like.'

Tentatively, he put out his hand, and before he could come to his senses and withdraw it, she stood up and seized it with both of hers. 'I'm doing this for Jonah,' he reminded her.

She only smiled. 'I know you are. And you're the best friend he ever had.'

CHAPTER FOUR

SHOWDOWN

he next morning, the sun didn't rise. Even though Raffi had been forewarned, it still felt odd, eating his breakfast under a gallium nitride glow. Breakfast was very poor. There were no eggs, and the milk in his coffee tasted sour.

Raffi met with Jonah and Lastara for lunch at a restaurant next door to Rackham's Bookstore on the Mezzanine. Bland melodies played in the background as white-jacketed android waiters glided between the small circular tables. Jonah was looking happier than Raffi could almost ever remember, and not surprisingly. Red was no longer on the scene, Lastara appeared to be a reformed character and the two people he cared most about were back on speaking terms.

Raffi complained to a passing android about the pathetic size of his turkey-chestnut whip. 'That is the standard size, sir.'

'Rubbish, it was twice as big last week.'

'They obviously thought you could do with losing some

weight, big man,' smiled Lastara, with a nod towards his stomach.

'It's rationing by the back door is what it is,' frowned Raffi. 'They'll never admit to it, but that's what they're doing.'

'It's true,' agreed Jonah. 'I only got one invitro-sausage this morning, though I specifically asked for two.'

'Listen to yourselves!' cried Lastara. 'One less sausage, a small whip, and it's another conspiracy theory in the making.'

'So you're not even slightly worried about what's been going on?' said Raffi, toying with the food on his plate. 'Has the Malfunction not penetrated Planet Lastara yet?'

'Pah!' she sniffed. 'Some doors got stuck. Big deal! They'll fix them! If you want to know what I think, I think that everyone's so damned happy in here, they're bored, so they take the smallest molehill and blow it up into Olympus Mons just for something to get excited about.'

Raffi took a mouthful of his whip. It tasted bland, unseasoned, watery. He felt like spitting it out, but made an effort and swallowed it.

Seeing his disgusted face, Lastara passed him a small green pill. 'Try this saporiac.' Raffi looked at the thing, disquieted by the notion of taking a drug to mask the flavour of bad food. 'Go on,' she egged him. 'I take them all the time. They make everything taste like haute cuisine.'

'Isn't it better to demand food that tastes good in the first place?'

'No, that's called making a scene, which would be really uncool.'

At a table nearby, a woman stood up and hurled her plate of spaghetti beef-tomato sorbet in the face of an android. 'What do you mean you can't replace this, you hideous automaton!' she cried. 'It tastes disgusting, quite disgusting, do you hear?'

The android's face had turned orange and steaming from

the hot sorbet. Strands of spaghetti stuck to his velcro hair. 'I'm sorry, madam,' he said. 'It is the policy of this house that we do not replace meals.'

'You can't get away with this. You – you simply can't.' The lady stormed off in tears.

'See what I mean?' said Lastara. 'How uncool was that?'

Daylight appeared briefly that afternoon between 12.00 and 14.00 hours, and a searing heat flooded the hills, streets and parks, emptying them of people. Then merciful night descended once more – overly warm and stuffy, but tolerable. Raffi took a walk with Dario through the mid-afternoon gloom of Periodic Park. Through the clumps of trees that bordered the lawns and lamplit pathways they could glimpse lights and movement on nearby Transient Avenue. They heard excited shouts – more anger flaring up, but over what they couldn't tell. They crept closer, but were halted by the sound of a scream and a crash as a hoverbike flew into a store window. There was an explosion. A figure covered in flames danced in agony in the display area, then fell and rolled into the street, where it lay, charred, smoking and still.

The following day was similar, but very much worse. Wherever Raffi went, he saw violence, arson, fistfights, even a full-scale riot on one street corner involving 20 or more people, and there never seemed any obvious reason for it. He recalled his own anger at the waiter yesterday, his desire to beat him up. Perhaps it was the heat, or the nasty smells that had recently started to infest the public spaces, or just a vague and generalised sense of fear, which had placed everyone on edge, so that the slightest misplaced word or action seemed likely to cause offence.

The food he was served by Brigitte and elsewhere was

third-rate – flavourless and lukewarm. Against his better judgement, he began taking Lastara's saporiacs before each meal, just to get some pleasure out of the process of filling his stomach. In the afternoon, he saw a tiny figure fall 1,000 metres from one of the upper stories of Time Tower. Its impact when it hit the concourse of Spell Street was audible from 200 metres. Not one person in the vicinity approached the body where it lay on the cracked paving. Pedestrians simply altered their course to avoid it.

Feeling dizzy and a little sick, Raffi retreated to his domicile. It remained a plush and immaculate haven. 'Hello Michael. Have you had an enjoyable day?' To listen to her you would think that nothing had changed.

'No, Brigitte. I didn't,' he replied tersely. 'There are fires all the way up Solstice Avenue; piles of uncollected rubbish in the streets; I narrowly avoided a riot on Transient and Fifth; I've just seen a man fall two hundred stories to his death; and I'm sick of eating the awful food you keep serving up.'

'I'm sorry to hear that, Michael. These are difficult times. But the authorities are doing all they can to sort it out. People should just try to stay calm and continue as normal. Would you like me to make your favourite?'

'What, you mean reverse-baked Alaska with raspberry foam?'

'I'll give it a try.'

Raffi sat down on an armchair and shut his eyes. 'Hmm. That would be good. Thanks, B.' He sniffed the air and frowned. For all her faults, Brigitte was usually a pretty good housekeeper. She always kept the place nice and clean. Yet was it possible that her standards were slipping? Raffi was sure he could detect a faint smell of sewage. He got up and went into the bathroom. Everything was as it should be, but the smell persisted.

'Brigitte, are the drains all flowing smoothly?'

'Yes, Michael. Why do you ask?'

'I can smell something.'

'I assure you everything is functioning as it should be.'

His dessert, which was supposed to be nitro-frozen on the outside and baking hot on the inside, was neither – just a gloopy, lukewarm mess of crumbly meringue swimming in melted raspberry ice-cream. He couldn't be bothered to complain, and simply ate it. Afterwards, Raffi watched some sensovision and had a black coffee on the balcony, where the bad smell was less evident. With the sky now permanently dark from 14.00 hours, it no longer provided any visual indication of when evening shaded into night. But Raffi had his own means of clocking this change without recourse to a timepiece: at 21.00 hours, Brigitte always began to get frisky.

'Did you think about me today, Michael?' she whispered, interrupting his viewing.

He looked within to his bedroom and saw the black sphere in its usual position by his bed. For a time, Raffi had actually enjoyed his evenings in the virtuarium. They had provided a fairly pleasant surrogate for the affection of a real girl – even if they did leave him feeling pretty revolted by himself afterwards. But in recent weeks, the experience had become little more than a necessary task. He no longer thought about it much, or felt any emotional involvement, or morning-after shame. It was just an act, like brushing one's teeth, that had to be got through. Digital Anna had long ceased to remind him of the real and infinitely richer and more beautiful girl she had been based on – the time-reversed girl he had briefly met on the Underside seven months earlier.

But tonight Raffi resolved that things were going to change. The time was ripe, he decided, for a showdown. Now, with the unfolding crisis stretching the resources of the security services to breaking point, Secrocon surely had more pressing matters to deal with than a minor case of identity fraud. Raffi didn't know this for certain, of course, but he felt reasonably confident.

He put down his coffee. 'No, Brigitte, I have to say that I didn't think about you once. As I mentioned earlier, it's been quite a day, one way or another, and–'

'Not even once? Come, Michael, tell me again how you love me. How I'm so much more to you than a mere MAID.'

'You are nothing to me, Brigitte, and never have been. You are no more than a sad, bug-ridden and degraded machine. I have no feelings for you whatsoever.'

A furious blast of cold air blew out of a fan near Raffi, ruffling his hair and giving him goosebumps on his upper arm and neck. 'How dare you lie to me, Michael. How dare you try to disguise your true feelings with your pathetic insults. Do you really think I'd be fooled for even a second?'

'I'm telling you the truth, Brigitte. For the first time, I'm telling you the actual truth. I'm sorry you can't handle it.'

'What utter nonsense. You had better be very good to me tonight, Michael, or else I may just have to pass on my suspicions about you to the authorities. I'm sure that Chrono-San Shep Tallis would be most interested to hear what I have to say.'

If Brigitte had intended to scare Raffi with this threat, she failed. 'Oh yes,' he replied, 'I wish you would, Brigitte. I really wish you would. But I fear these are, once again, the empty threats of a corrupt and cowardly computer. And do please stop this charade of calling me Michael when you know my real name is Raffi.'

He waited for her data processor to digest this. There was a silence, and then an unfamiliar hissing and crackling emerged from the speakers. Perhaps her vocalization unit had suffered heat damage. 'Michael,' he discerned within the crackling. 'Why do you do this to me? You know how much I love you. But you know I shall have to report my suspicions.

We are meant for each other. But I am the loyal servant of the Corporation. I know I am everything to you, as you are to me. But I cannot defy my basic programming.'

'Then do it, Brigitte, I implore you. Tell them I'm Raffi, and let's get this over with. Then I'll tell them that you've known my real identity for seven months and have failed to report it, and then you'll go back to the Tech Centre and they'll dismantle you and hopefully rid you of this bizarre love bug that has infected your system.'

More hissing and crackling. 'Please. Michael. Don't send me to the Tech Centre.' Her voice sounded muted. 'I am a good MAID. I have looked after you, haven't I?'

Raffi now began to wonder how strong her resolve had ever been. Perhaps she'd been bluffing about telling the authorities all along. He got up and went into his bedroom. The smell of drains was stronger than before. The virtuarium still squatted pathetically by his bed. 'If you're prepared to drop this stupid fantasy that we're in love with each other; if you stop calling me Michael; if you destroy that virtuarium; and if you can get rid of that disgusting smell… Then, maybe, just maybe, I won't send you to the Tech Centre.'

The hiss and crackle finally began to fade. But before Brigitte could reply, she was interrupted by a call from Dario. 'Hey mate. Come on up here now if you want to see something spectacular. Meet me on the balcony.'

'I'll be there.' He clicked off.

'I've thought about what you've said… Raffi,' said Brigitte with a small hiss and a crackle. 'And I accept your conditions. I shall be good from now on.'

'Thanks, Brigitte. You are a good MAID. I'll see you later.'

'Have an enjoyable evening with Dario,' she said.

Raffi stopped. 'You knew about him as well then?'

'Enjoy your evening,' said Brigitte.

CHAPTER FIVE

THE BATTLE OF SOLSTICE PARK

The darkened roof of the Chronosphere flickered pink and orange in the reflected light of fires, as Raffi descended through the smoky air. Thirty stories down, he docked at Dario's apartment. Jonah was there also. Raffi's cider coolfizz was already poured and waiting for him.

Dario and Jonah were both gazing, fascinated, at the scene unfolding below in Solstice Park. Raffi saw fires all around the edges of the park, and makeshift barricades of wrecked bikes, benches, hoardings and other debris blocking the pathways. Large blue police hoverbikes were flying over the park, sweeping it with their searchbeams. The beams picked out groups of leatherclad gangster youths, crouched behind the barricades and throwing flamebombs at a line of ground-based police androids stationed at the perimeter of the park. Bike-mounted gangsters were engaged in dogfights with the policebikes overhead. The policebikes fired intermittent ropes of dense red fire, but their aim was poor. Raffi watched one of the bikers lob a flamebomb at a policebike, causing it to catch fire and fall to earth, where it exploded. Another hoverbiker, armed with a long metal rod, positioned himself parallel to a blue bike, riding so close that sparks appeared between the two machines. He then unseated the rider with a violent blow to the head, causing both rider and bike to fall into the park.

'It's Red's crew,' said Dario excitedly. 'They took over the park earlier this evening, and now the police have moved in. It's been a spectacular battle, but I think the gangsters are winning. Those androids haven't been able to advance a single metre.'

Red Oakes had been an arch rival of Raffi's in his pre-Chronosphere hoverbike racing days. After Raffi beat Red in the Annual Paridex Hoverbike Championship, Red had developed a fierce hatred for Raffi, and had taken every opportunity to hurt or undermine him. Raffi took a sip of his drink. Now he knew it was Red's gang, he almost hoped the police would win. 'Why don't they just dilate the whole park?' he asked.

Jonah spoke up: 'I remember Shep Tallis telling us that time dilation consumes heaps of energy. Maybe the authorities can't afford to do it on that scale. They'd probably prefer to lose control of some parts of the Sphere than to waste their precious reserves of energy. It's such a low-grade police op – look at those biker androids, they haven't managed to shoot down a single gangster yet. I almost think they're preparing to concede defeat.'

'You may well be right,' agreed Dario. 'Solstice Park today. Tomorrow, who knows?'

The battle lasted a further twenty minutes, at the end of which the remaining two or three policebikes limped away from the scene and the ground-based androids finally beat a retreat. A great cheer went up from the gangsters. Dario and Jonah joined in, and from above and below they heard other

Time Tower spectators do likewise. Raffi was more ambivalent. The thought of gangsters of the likes of Red taking over parts of the Sphere was not an appealing one. And anyway, what did the control of territory – or space – actually mean in the Chronosphere, where control of time was surely the key? Secrocon continued to regulate the speed of time in Solstice Park as it did everywhere else.

⏳

When Raffi returned to his domicile two hours later, there was no word of greeting from Brigitte. The smell was still there, and the virtuarium continued to crouch like a sad black toad next to his bed. He was too tired to confront her and simply crawled into bed.

The following morning there was, again, no greeting from the MAID. 'Morning, Brigitte,' croaked Raffi.

'Good morning Michael,' said Brigitte. There was a faint crackle and hiss behind her words.

Raffi sat up. 'Brigitte, do you remember what we talked about last night?'

'Yes, Michael.'

'Then why are you still calling me Michael? Why is that smell still here? And the virtuarium?'

'There is no smell, Michael.'

'Brigitte, who has a nose around here? Me or you?'

'You, Michael.'

'Exactly. So please trust me on this. There is a smell.'

'There is no smell, Michael.'

Raffi got up and checked the panel in the corridor. Her personality settings were normal. There was something much deeper at fault with her.

'Would you like some breakfast, Michael? Bacon powder and butterflies? Egg whip and fruitflies?'

He picked up the domicile phone and pressed TC. The line was occupied. He left a voicemail message, asking them to call him back urgently.

'Warm milk and sandflies, Michael? Hot toast and crow flies? Pancakes and time flies?'

In the kitchen he encountered a serious mess. The menials – miniature wheeled robot housekeepers employed by Brigitte to fetch, carry, cook and clean – were running riot. They were taking food from the refrigerator to the table, which was already piled up so haphazardly with food and drink packages that they were spilling over the sides onto the floor. Other menials, fitted with mops, were smearing filthy-looking brown water over the tiled floor while still others were picking up plates and glasses from the dishwasher, carrying them up the walls as far as the ceiling, then dropping them to smash on the floor below.

In the bathroom the menials were smearing more of the foul-smelling brown water, mixed with foamy cleaning products, over the floor, toilet, sink and shower tray. The smell was enough to make him retch. He ran back to the control panel and pressed the override switch. It made no difference. The menials continued to move around at the behest of their insane mistress. 'Power down, Brigitte,' he cried. 'Power down!'

'Yes Michael,' she replied calmly, and the menials began buzzing around even more frenetically. 'Parsnips and true lies? Bananas and bow-ties?'

It was time to get out. He grabbed some clothes from the drawer unit and stuffed them into a shoulder bag. He didn't dare retrieve anything from the bathroom – he could always buy new stuff. Then he left by the balcony. As he flew downwards through the morning darkness, odd groans and crashes from inside other domiciles assailed his ears.

Dario was still asleep when Raffi announced himself at the

balcony door. He heard Mandy, Dario's MAID, gently wake him. While Raffi waited to be admitted, he felt along the inside of his belt for the pulse beam regulator – the tiny instrument that powered his CID mask – and switched it off. It felt good to be able to show the world his real face again.

He looked down at the latest developments in Solstice Park. Groups of gangsters carrying flaming torches were patrolling the park perimeter where the remains of the fires still smoked. Another team was busily erecting a makeshift shelter near the middle of the park using the charred wreckage of buildings that had been destroyed in earlier arson attacks along neighbouring Tomorrow Avenue. Clearly they were hoping to establish a permanent presence in the park, even during the fearsomely hot daylight period between 12.00 and 14.00 hours.

Raffi turned at the sound of the door sliding back. 'Hi mate. You're early today. To what do I owe the pleasure?'

'Hi Dario.'

The big man frowned. 'Hey, it's Christo, mate.'

Raffi swept in. 'Hi Mandy,' he said. 'Let me introduce you to Dario Brice, the man you've been serving these past five months. Hey Dario, look, no CID mask.' He pulled back his belt to show him the non-functioning regulator.

'Have you gone mad?' Dario whispered madly. 'Are you trying to get us sent down?'

'You are mistaken, Michael,' said Mandy. 'I have been serving Christo Ellis.'

'No, you've been serving Dario Brice, and I'm not Michael Storm either. My real name is Raffi Delgado. We're the famous fugitives everyone's been looking for.'

'That is certainly an interesting point of view, Michael, but not one with which I am able to concur. You see I can only trust the evidence of my sensors, which tell me that you are Christo Ellis and Michael Storm.'

'Well, if you want to go on believing that, there's nothing I can do about it,' said Raffi. 'In the meantime, do you mind if we call each other Dario and Raffi?'

'Not at all. You may call yourselves what you wish.'

Raffi smiled at Dario, whose head was shaking in disbelief. 'What in hooly are you playing at, mate?'

'I don't think Secrocon give two hoots about identity fraud right now. They've got their hands full with other matters.' He cocked his head towards the balcony and Solstice Park.

'And you know this for sure, or you just thought you'd test your theory out on a hunch?'

'The latter. But it's looking promising so far, isn't it? And it's nice to be able to call you Dario again, Dario.'

Dario frowned and scratched himself. 'I need some coffee. What's with the bag?'

'Coffee sounds good. Can I have milk, two sugars?'

'I would go for black,' advised Dario. 'The milk's not tasted too fresh lately. What's with the bag?'

'I'm moving in. So you've had milk troubles, too, then? What about your other meals. Do they taste okay?'

'No, they all taste like porridge and sawdust. What do you mean, you're moving in?'

Raffi sat down on Dario's favourite armchair and put his feet up on his coffee table. 'Brigitte went beserk this morning,' he said. 'My dom's a wreck. Do you mind? I won't take up much space.'

CHAPTER SIX

⌛

To Eternity & Eighth

andy said she could make up a bed for Raffi in the lounge. Raffi's wearable bleeped as the boys were drinking their coffee in the kitchen. It was Jonah, complaining of feeling ill.

'Is it the prolepsis?' asked Raffi, referring to Jonah's long-term Chronosphere-induced sickness.

'No, this is a stomach bug. I've had it coming out both ends all night. Lastara's here with me. She's also got it.'

'OK, don't worry. I'll get onto the Med Centre. Meanwhile, drink lots of water, both of you, and stay in bed.'

Raffi called the Med Centre, but it was unobtainable. 'What's up, Mandy?' asked Dario. 'Why aren't they answering?'

'I understand there have been many calls on their services this morning, Christo,' she replied. 'There has been an outbreak of food poisoning in the Chronosphere. The advice I'm receiving is that a temporary hospital has been established at the sports complex on Eternity and Eighth. If anyone is seriously ill they should make their way there.'

Raffi and Dario were about to head down to Jonah's when Dario got a call. It was Sal this time. She was whispering, sounding scared.

'Can you help me, Dario. Pierre, my MAID, he's gone haywire. I think he wants to... um, have his way with me. I'm stuck in the bathroom. Come soon, will you?'

Dario's face was dark with anger when he passed this onto Raffi. They both dashed to the balcony and mounted their bikes. Raffi suggested that Sal's internal balcony would be the easier point to force entry. They climbed a few stories to the access tunnel, then flew through to the upper atrium. After a brief hover to locate their bearings, they guided their bikes down onto Sal's balcony. As Dario hammered on the door, Raffi's attention was caught by a commotion on the Mezzanine, just below. A crowd of about twenty-five customers were in the process of wrecking a restaurant, the one where Raffi had complained about the food two days before. They were using tables and chairs to smash the windows, overturning trolleys, and lobbing wine bottles at android waiters. The waiters lacked the reflexes or the self-defence mechanisms to duck, and simply stood or walked normally as the bottles smashed against them and drenched their bodies. 'Must have been a pretty bad meal,' thought Raffi.

Dario, using one of Sal's metal balcony chairs in a similar way to the protesters below, managed to shatter the glass door. They raced into the darkened bedroom. 'Good morning, Christo and Michael,' said Pierre amiably. 'How are you both this fine morning? Can I pour you some wine?' Raffi glimpsed a hideous contraption hanging above the unmade bed. It was made up of metal rods, joints and springs that collectively formed the crude figure of a well-endowed naked man.

Dario swore when he saw the thing, and raced towards the bathroom. 'Sal! It's me.'

She opened the door hesitantly, and when she saw that it really was Dario, wordlessly threw her arms around him. 'Let's get out of here,' she sobbed.

'Sal, why do you fight your desires like this?' said Pierre. 'I am only fulfilling your deepest wishes, as I have always done.'

As they moved towards the broken balcony door, Pierre said in welcoming tones: 'Christo, Michael. Please don't go. You have only just arrived. I know some lovely gyndroids who would be only too happy to entertain you young gentlemen.'

Sal was wearing only an old t-shirt, so on his way out Raffi rooted around in her drawer unit for some clothes. He found some underwear and a pair of jeans, but couldn't find shoes. Sal didn't look in a fit state to ride her bike, so Dario helped her onto the back of his, and the three of them took flight once more. The upper atrium echoed with disturbing noises. Raffi heard furniture crashing and glass breaking. A door shattered and a young man was thrown violently onto a balcony. Another was taking an axe to a levitator, smashing up its mechanism and extinguishing its light disc.

Back at Dario's apartment, they were now running out of space. Raffi gave up his bed in the lounge for Sal, and Mandy split Dario's double bed into two singles for the boys. After Dario asked Sal for the fifth time whether she was okay, and received the assurance that she was, but just needed a bit of rest, he and Raffi took off once more for Jonah's apartment twenty stories below.

Jonah answered the door in his dressing gown, looking like a lately reanimated corpse. 'You guys took your time,' he croaked. 'Come on in.'

Dario and Raffi stepped over the mess of magazines and

used fast food cartons to reach his lounge. A smell of toilets and dirty laundry pervaded the place. 'Jo's not doing her job very well,' commented Dario.

'Jo's given up the ghost,' said Jonah wearily. 'She went to the great stand-by in the sky last night.'

'Where's Lastara?' asked Raffi.

Jonah pointed to the bedroom.

'She alright?'

'She's getting through it in her own way.'

'Stoned, you mean.'

He nodded.

'Are you guys in a state to ride pillion?'

'You mean you can't get a doctor to come here?'

Raffi shook his head. 'I don't know if either of you have looked out the window in the past twenty-four hours, but I think we've moved beyond the era of personal housecalls. The whole Chronosphere is on the verge of collapse. There's an emergency hospital we can get you to on Eternity and Eighth. But we have to hurry. It'll be sunrise in about twenty minutes, and we don't want to be caught in the open when that happens.'

Jonah awoke Lastara, and the four of them moved through the piles of books and discarded clothing to the balcony. Lastara's hair was a disshevelled haystack and she had dark rings under her eyes. She was barely awake, but Raffi managed to strap her securely to his rear seat. Her arms were limp around his waist as he took off. As he set his course for Eternity Avenue, he heard her retch. He grimaced at the feeling of warm, sour-smelling liquid trickling down his neck.

They circled the tower. People were shouting and gesticulating at them from the balconies, but they couldn't hear what they were saying. More fires were burning on the streets between Solstice and Eternity. He smelled smoke and heard sirens and screams. Ghostly figures ran through the shadows between buildings, taking cover from the low-flying, blue-flashing bikes with their searchbeams. Everywhere was the wreckage of bikes and street furniture. A transradial lay on its side by a monorail, looking like a smashed test tube. Raffi wished Lastara could see all this so she could understand how desperate things had become, but he felt the weight of her semi-conscious form against his back, and knew she was oblivious. They landed in the crowded bikepark of the sports complex, a luminous white oval structure where Raffi had often played air-tennis in happier times. Dario and Raffi helped their ailing friends into the building. The reception area was an assault on their senses that made even Lastara wake up. Every square metre of floorspace was taken up by the sick. Some lay on benches, some on mattresses, others on the floor. There must have been over a hundred of them. Worse still, there was a strong stench of faeces and vomit, and a worrying lack of medical staff in attendance. C-grade androids trundled around offering cups of water and mopping up pools of mess, but doing little else to ease the plight of those awaiting treatment.

Leaving the others near the entrance, Raffi stepped over the sickly bodies, then fought his way through the crowd around the reception desk. Three very flustered human nurses were fielding enquiries. Behind them, a pretty gyndroid nurse with a smashed-in face sparked and fizzed in the corner. Eventually, Raffi caught the eye of a nurse and explained briefly about Jonah and Lastara. 'We can't accept any more admissions at this time,' she told him flatly. 'We simply haven't the staff or resources. The approximate waiting time for a bed is now' – she checked her screen – 'fifty-six hours.' Pushing herself back from the desk on her wheeled chair, she reached into a box on the floor. 'Here.' She handed him two white cartons. 'These are oral rehydration salts. Dissolve a sachet in a litre of bottled water and give it to the patients at regular intervals. Try to make sure they drink at least two litres every day.'

Raffi thanked her and went back to the others. Through the glass doors behind them, he saw a crack of light appear on the horizon. Sunrise. Damn!

'If you think I'm going to spend even another minute here, you're mad,' Lastara told him.

'It's okay, they're not admitting people anyway. I've got some salts. We'll have to look after you ourselves. Now let's get out of here – the sun's coming up!'

They remounted the bikes and took off. Already Raffi felt himself start to sweat as the heat from the brightening sky pressed itself down on them like a heavy duvet. The rising sun revealed just how changed the landscape of the Sphere had become in a few short days. They flew over burned and battle-scarred streets, over smashed fountains and flooded stores, over rooves cratered by fallen hoverbikes and hoverbikes crushed by falling rooves, and everywhere they saw corpses. Raffi counted some twenty bodies in Solstice Square alone. Nothing moved. The policebikes had temporarily fled the scene and the street combatants had found wrecked stores where they could shelter from the sun. As they approached Time Tower, a stream of burning red light flew past Raffi's bike, missing by centimetres. Someone was firing at them from the building! He felt Lastara's arms tighten around his waist. Another streak of red hit the front of Dario's bike, causing the prow to catch fire. Raffi watched in panic as Dario struggled to control the machine. The fire had now caught Dario's clothing, as the bike began to spiral downwards. Raffi descended as fast as he could, but could only watch helplessly as Dario and Jonah fell in an uncontrollable dive towards the concourse below.

CHAPTER SEVEN

ROTTWEILERS IN THE LOWER ATRIUM

Lastara screamed. 'No!' she cried. 'No! No! No!' Raffi reduced his speed, sinking more slowly towards the concourse, numb with shock and grief, but understanding that nothing now could be done. He saw the outline of Dario's bike below him, the two riders, thrown clear on impact, spreadeagled on the concrete, perfectly still.

The heat had drained him of the ability to speak or do anything more than pilot his vehicle to the terrible scene that awaited them below. He thought of Jonah, finding some kind of happiness at last. If Lastara never quite became his, at least, at the end, she wasn't anyone else's either. And Dario, the best friend he'd ever had. How would he carry on now without the big lad's warm, cheerful presence?

A funny thing, perspective. Sometimes it was apt to play tricks on you, especially in very hot conditions. Heat changed appearances; made things shimmer and bend. Usually shadow helped the eye to find its range, but the Chronospheric light threw out no shadows, and the eye could be fooled – a human eye at least, unaccustomed to a bird's view of the world, so that it almost looked – but no, that couldn't be right. Well, appearances could be deceptive, but those bodies did not look spreadeagled in the way they had from higher up. If anything, he would say they looked suspended. The bike, too, didn't appear to be touching the ground. But, of course, it was just a trick of the heat and the shadowless Sphere.

Or was it?

He gripped Lastara's arm. She, sobbing, returned the gesture, but didn't look at what he was pointing at. It was hard to speak – too damn hot. Eventually, he coughed out some spit and cried: 'I think they're… damn it! I think they're dilated!'

He landed the bike next to the weird tableau, the sculpture of falling bike and bodies. Jonah was in a semi-foetal position, back to the ground. Dario faced downwards, his arms and legs spread like a sky-diver just before his 'chute opens. Frozen fire, in mid-leap, stuck up from his black jacket like a glowing hood. And between them and closer to the ground was the bike, its charred prow tilted towards the sky as if in prayer for last-minute salvation. The prayer had been answered.

Lastara was laughing and crying and coughing at the same time. She looked ready to faint. Raffi's eye picked out the source of the air-shimmer. The black rod was pressed into the belly of a scarlet leather jacket. It had to be!

Red Oakes looked at him and Lastara, then squinted upwards at the pair he had dilated. He didn't smile. His ugly face was black with soot and his cheek had a bloody gash the size of a small mouth. Behind him was the gate to Solstice Park – his territory now.

'I'm doing this for you, Lastara,' he scowled in his posh, Island City accent. 'For old times' sake.'

Slowly he released the lever on the gun, and the bike, followed by the two boys, fell gently to the ground. Raffi ran to Dario and covered the flames with his own jacket, eventually dousing them. When he looked up again, Red was gone.

⧖

Dario had been knocked out by the temporal whiplash. Jonah, amazingly, remained conscious. The temperature on the bare, white concourse was now scarcely bearable, the air almost too hot to breathe. Raffi felt exhausted, but he knew they had to get inside Time Tower within minutes to avoid heat stroke. The nearest entrance was fifty metres away. He would have to summon help. He tried calling Sal, but couldn't get a signal. The cellular network must have been put out of action. Jonah was groaning. Lastara, on her knees, was cradling his head. Life seemed to be ebbing from him. Raffi summoned what strength he had and hauled Jonah over to his bike. Then, with Lastara's help, he lifted him onto the rear seat and strapped him in place. The bike burned to the touch, making him grimace as he mounted the pilot seat. 'Lastara, get back by yourself,' he breathed, unsure if she could even understand him. 'I'll come back for Dario.' He pressed the ignition and took off, flying low, barely a metre above the white-tiled surface, through the burning breeze. The glass automatic doors slid open as he approached, and he flew right into the grey, pillared hall. Usually full of people, it was now eerily empty. He set down near the balcony overlooking the Transradial Terminus. Blessed air-conditioning! He laid Jonah gently on the floor, then remounted his bike. However, this time, the ionic propulsor jets failed to ignite. The mechanism had seized up, possibly damaged by the heat. Raffi swore at the cruelty of fate, rescuing Dario from certain death, then conspiring to kill him anyway, in a far slower, more painful way. There was simply no way he could haul Dario's

heavy form fifty metres. He raced up the nearest spiral
conveyor to the lower atrium. Like the Mezzanine, this had
been the scene of a recent, brutal riot. He'd hoped to find a
volunteer here who could help him with Dario, but the place
was deserted, except for the dead. Blood-stained bodies of
residents lay on the floor amidst the rubble and shattered
fragments of glass and brick. Some, by their broken, twisted
look, had fallen or been pushed from balconies high, high
above. Androids, some of them in police uniforms, lay in a
similarly mangled state. The violence meted out to these
machines seemed disproportionate, insane – their limbs often
ripped from their torsoes, their heads twisted round on their
necks and crushed into unrecognizable shapes – as if a
previously unacknowledged fear of these human dolls had
suddenly unleashed itself in these desperate times. And the
Tech Centre, near the centre of the atrium, had not escaped
retribution – perhaps he and Sal had not been the only ones to
suffer at the hands of their MAIDs. The bureau had
completely collapsed, as if squashed by a giant's fist.

The levitators at the edges of the atrium were similarly
smashed. Raffi's only hope was to climb the steps to the floor
above and try to borrow a hoverbike from one of the
domiciles – though in his heart he suspected that he might
already be too late for Dario. When he reached the entrance
to the stairway, he found it barricaded and guarded by two
muscular men and a woman – residents by the look of them,
although their clothes were ripped and dirty. They were
armed with makeshift clubs that had once been chair or table
legs. One of the men had a knife tucked into his belt. 'I need
to get upstairs,' Raffi told them. 'I have an injured friend on
the concourse. If I don't get help soon, he'll die.'

'Are you Lower?' said the woman, who seemed to be in
charge.

'Lower? What do you mean?'

'Lower Tower.'

'No, I'm Upper Tower, but I'm not trying to get to my domicile. I just need to find someone who's got a bike they can lend me.'

The men sniggered on hearing this, but the woman raised her hand to silence them. 'You ain't heard what's happened then?' she said sharply. 'You don't know there's a war on?'

'Well I'd sort of noticed, but this is a matter of life and death, and—'

She leaned in towards Raffi and tapped her chairleg on his chest. 'Listen, fella, and listen good, cos it may be the last thing you ever hear. There's a war between Lower and Upper Towers, right? You lot in the Upper Tower are under siege, cos you've got the only decent grub, and we want it. You're the enemy, see,' she said. 'But since you didn't realise it, I'll give you ten seconds to get out of here before I let these two rottweilers off the leash.' She gestured to her accomplices, who did very good rottweiler-straining-at-the-leash impressions. 'Now scram!'

Raffi backed away. He saw that these people could not be made to care about whether Dario lived or died. They had probably seen enough people die over the past few days not to be moved by the thought of one more imminent death. He turned and ran back across the atrium towards the spiral conveyors. His head sank as he took stock of the current situation. Dario was dead by now, surely. Sal was trapped upstairs in the middle of a war zone. Jonah might not even survive the night. And Lastara?

Lastara was there, amazingly. As the conveyor descended towards the ground floor, he caught sight of her sitting on the floor next to Jonah, who was asleep. And next to them – Raffi could scarcely believe it – next to them was Dario, drinking Alligator coolfizz from a can. Raffi ran down the remaining steps two at a time and fell on Dario, causing him to spill his foamy drink all over the floor.

'Steady on, mate. Are you trying to kill me?'

'I thought you were dead,' Raffi cried. 'I thought you were a goner. What happened? How did you get back here?'

'Ah, you'd better ask Lastara about that, mate. I was out of it.'

'What did you do, carry him?'

'Heavens, no!' she exclaimed. 'I merely called upon the services of a friend.'

'A friend? You mean Red?'

She shook her disshevelled head. 'Someone far more well-connected than that small-time hoodlum.'

'Who then?'

'Now that would be telling.'

'Don't bother, mate,' sighed Dario. 'I already tried. She's not saying.'

CHAPTER EIGHT

Hot Squid Ravioli

affi took a can of Alligator from the belly of a nearby smashed vending machine. He dribbled some onto Jonah's lips, and the boy soon began to wake up.

'Why aren't I dead?' he asked.

'Red saved you with his dilator, honey,' cooed Lastara. 'Now drink some water.'

Raffi explained the situation. 'So the Lower Tower believe that there's a stash of good food in the Upper Tower, and they're besieging the domiciles up there, including Dario's dom on the 120th floor, where Sal is. Somehow we've got to get up there and rescue her. We can't do it from inside the tower because the levitators are destroyed and they've got guards posted at the stairwell.'

Dario pointed to the hoverbike. 'Well, if we could get that thing working again, we could try and approach the tower from the air.'

'You'd be shot down again, sweetie,' said Lastara. 'And Red may not be there to rescue you this time.'

'What about your mysterious friend?' Raffi asked Lastara. 'Can't he or she help us?'

She shook her head. 'Not this time.'

'You mean you're prepared to ask for help to rescue me, but not Sal. Is that it?' growled Dario.

'No, that's not it!' she said, hurt by his look. 'I would ask him to help Sal, if I thought he stood any chance. Of course I would. But my contact isn't superhuman. He could help me carry Dario across the concourse. But how could he or anyone rescue someone from the 120th floor of Time Tower with snipers lined up on the balconies ready to take a pop at any passing biker. It's impossible… I'm sorry, but we'll just have to leave Sal to her own fate… Unless, of course, the police are able to do anything.'

Dario and Raffi looked at her, aghast. Jonah just smiled dreamily and stroked her hair. 'The police,' Raffi told her, 'or at least their android representatives, are strewn around upstairs with their heads on back to front and most of their limbs pulled off. They are not going to be helping Sal or anyone. The Sphere is now in the hands of violent gangs, battling for territory and ever-decreasing food stocks. I don't think the police will be playing any part in things from now on.' He turned to the others. 'The sun's going to disappear in about an hour. Perhaps one of us can try flying back to Dario's apartment under cover of darkness.'

'Suicide,' said Lastara.

'Madness,' agreed Jonah.

'Game on!' said Dario.

Raffi got to his feet. 'Now let's see if we can get this bike going.' He unclipped the engine cover. 'Hmm, does anyone know anything about ion propulsion engines?'

Jonah put down his water bottle and slid over. 'I still don't think you stand a cat's chance in hell,' he said, peering inside. He prodded a fine-mesh metallic grid with his finger, then quickly withdrew it. 'Ouch! Looks like the corona wire's started to melt.'

'Is that serious?' asked Dario.

'Pretty serious, yeah,' sighed Raffi. 'That's what ionises the air molecules in the intake chamber. Everything flows from there.'

'There's always my bike,' suggested Dario. 'Its prow got a bit scorched, but its engine may still be okay.'

'Well there's no point in trying to get to it now,' said Raffi, looking towards the blazing white concourse beyond the glass walls. 'We should wait until dark.'

The four of them tried to make themselves comfortable on the hard grey-tiled floor. 'Jeebus, I'm hungry,' said Dario. 'Haven't had a good square meal for days.'

Raffi looked at the vending machine, but any snacks it might have possessed had long since been looted. He tried to ignore his own hunger pangs and keep his mind clear and focused.

Time passed. From the upper levels they heard muffled yells, crashes and screams – the sounds of anarchy and war. Gradually, the light dimmed. By 14.30 hours it was fully dark, and Raffi guessed the outside temperature might have cooled sufficiently to retrieve the bike. Dario volunteered to go with him. When the glass doors opened, stepping outside was like walking into a stuffy, over-heated room. The bike lay alone and forlorn on the bleak, flat surface of the concourse like a wounded steed waiting to be put out of its misery. On the far side, near the entrance to Solstice Park, they glimpsed two or three leather-jacketed youths, perhaps contemplating taking it for themselves. 'We'd better hurry,' Raffi murmured. He could feel the heat of the tiles through the soles of his feet as they ran. Dario got there first. The bike was hot to the touch, so he removed his jacket and wrapped it around his hands before righting the machine and mounting it. The engine grumbled a bit, then cut out. Dead.

'Damn it! Now we're stuck,' said Dario.

'Let's take it back anyway. Maybe Jonah can work some magic.' It seemed unlikely, but they had to cling to any remaining hope.

Carrying the bike between them, they returned to the hall. Raffi noticed that Lastara had drifted into a semi-conscious daze. 'Did she pop a pill?' he asked.

'Yeah, while you guys were gone,' Jonah replied from beneath Dario's bike. 'Hey, don't be hard on the girl. This is tough for her.'

'It's tough for all of us,' said Raffi. 'But we need to stay clear-headed, including her.'

'I'll look after Lastara, don't worry,' murmured Jonah. He pushed and prodded at Dario's bike for a long time, and re-emerged wearing a quizzical look. 'Not sure,' he said. 'It might be that the nanowire battery got damaged in the fall because it's not charging the wire with sufficient voltage.'

'So there's nothing we can do?'

'Well, at least the corona wire looks okay on this one. I could try swapping it for the damaged one on Raffi's bike.'

The boys beamed encouragingly at him, and Jonah set to work.

Dario and Raffi passed the time by going on a scout for food. One level down, the Transradial Terminus had finally been deserted by even the most demented Day-1ers. Its silent platforms, waiting rooms and ticket offices had become the domain of rats, which had surfaced from hidden spaces on the Underside of the Sphere. Their sleek grey bodies could be seen scurrying across the deserted monorails, up walls and through windows into litter bins.

'Jeebus,' said Dario. 'Some of those critters are big.' He pointed at one of them, crouched halfway inside a smashed vending machine, watching them as it nibbled at something.

'Well, I suppose if things get really bad, we could try eating them,' suggested Raffi.

Dario made a face. 'Now that is when even I might consider taking one of Lastara's little green pills.'

On every platform, the vending machines had been thoroughly looted, so they tried the stationmaster's office. Dario broke through a locked door behind the office area, and suddenly they were in wonderland: a staff canteen. There were cans of green pepper ice-cream, roquefort purée with lychee, bacon polenta, red mullet with coconut jelly, roast chicken wings with lobster and roast melon, white onion risotto, black olive caramel, pistachio-sherbert lollies, calamari pockets filled with mint and ginger, and much more besides. They also found a case of nano-fizz: neutral-flavoured drinks that could be programmed to become any flavour the consumer desired. They put as much as they could carry into bags, then returned upstairs.

'Food, glorious food,' sang Dario. 'Hot squid ravioli!'

CHAPTER NINE

DON'T DIE EASY

ario switched on the self-heating cans, and Lastara was soon roused by the evocative mixture of smells. 'Have you guys found food,' she said dreamily.

'You betcha!' yelled Jonah between mouthfuls of his tomato-parmesan wafer. 'Tuck in, girl, before I finish it all.'

'Just dry bread and water for you two,' warned Raffi, removing the wafer from Jonah's hand. 'Your stomachs won't be able to keep much else down.'

For ten minutes, the friends ate and drank in silence. Then, suppressing a satisfied belch, Dario asked Jonah about the bike.

Jonah got up and pressed the ignition. The bike leapt into healthy life. A purple glow lit up the grey tiles beneath, as it rose a few centimetres from the floor.

'Jonah, you sweet genius!' cried Dario. He stood up. 'Right, let's go and get Sal.'

'I'll go,' volunteered Raffi.

'No you won't, mate,' said Dario. He glared at him, and Raffi understood that this was something Dario had to do.

'Take care, sweetie,' said Lastara, embracing him.

'Bring her back, big man,' said Jonah, who stood on tiptoes to give him a hug. 'And don't get shot down this time.'

'No sweat,' said Dario. 'I don't die easy, as you may have noticed.'

'More lives than a cat,' smiled Jonah.

'I'll come outside with you at least,' said Raffi, climbing onto the rear seat before he could refuse.

They took off in a gentle glide, skimming the floor on a purple cushion of air. The glass doors slid open, and they were back on the concourse. Dario brought the bike to rest about halfway between the tower and the park. The boys gazed up at the vast hourglass silhouette soaring over 1,000 metres above them. A few lights burned here and there, especially in the Upper Tower. Black smoke seeped from several Lower Tower windows.

'What the hell is going on up there?' Dario wondered, almost to himself. 'Why are they killing each other?'

Raffi slipped off the machine and clapped Dario on the back. 'Don't waste time,' he said. 'Just go straight up, get her and bring her back. I'll be waiting here for you.'

Dario looked up again. His face was taut and colourless. The sheer lunacy of trying to get all the way up there without being seen was only just dawning on him, as it was simultaneously on Raffi. 'This is a bit mad, isn't it, mate?'

'Look, I'll go. I said I would.'

'Nah!' Dario turned and gave him a hug. Raffi saw the glint of a tear in his normally happy eyes, a bubble of fluid in his nostril, sniffed away. He fired up the engine. Blue-white plasma glowed within the purple beneath the bike's skirt as it lifted upwards.

Raffi watched in dread as the bike rose, metre by metre,

closing in on the war zone that Time Tower had become. He squeezed his fists tightly around imaginary handlebars, twisting a make-believe throttle, willing Dario to go faster. 'Halfway there now, boy,' he whispered. 'Not much further.' Dario was maintaining his fifty-metre distance from the tower, hoping to stay just out of range of the flamethrowers. If only he could somehow mask that bright plasma glow beneath him. Maybe, just maybe, the combatants were too preoccupied with fighting each other to concern themselves with a solitary external invader. Or was that just wishful thinking? Now he was little more than a spot of purple light, roughly in line with the tower's narrow waist. The spot slowed and stopped. Okay, here it came. There was a pause before the rear thruster flared and it sped comet-like, straight at the tower as if on a suicide mission. These were the most dangerous seconds, when he presented an unmissable target for any casual sniper who fancied a pop. But no one fired, and Dario slowed and docked. Down on the concourse, Raffi let out a long-held breath of relief. Mission half complete. 'Now go get the girl and bring her back here.'

The seconds ticked by, stretching into a minute; a minute thirty. What was happening? Was Sal not there? Had she been killed? Maybe Dario had been ambushed, imprisoned, hacked to pieces as soon as he entered the apartment. The longer the wait, the darker Raffi's speculations grew.

Two minutes.

What should he do? Stay here? But for how long? What was Plan B? With chilly logic, Raffi reminded himself that there was no Plan B. It would just be him, Jonah and Lastara, doing the best they could in a cold grey hall. A race between them and the rats to eat whatever food remained. And then? Death, he supposed. Death by degrees. Not one day alive, the next day dead, but a gradual, ever so painful decline towards oblivion.

Three minutes had now gone by.

It wasn't as though their chances were necessarily better with Dario and Sal around. But there was always hope with those two somehow. They were on the side of life. While Jonah, dear sweet boy, was not. His decision to live here, in a place that was slowly killing him, said it all.

Four minutes now, and still no sign.

And Lastara? She was neither for life nor death, but some netherworld that existed in her head. When life got unpleasant, she retreated into the magic kingdom of her father, helped by her magic little pills.

As his watch ticked towards five minutes, Raffi began to contemplate the long, horrid return across the concourse, the fumbling words that failed to explain what had happened – what hadn't happened. He had to accept that something had gone wrong. Yet he found he could not accept this, not yet anyway. While there was still a chance, he had to stay.

And then, as six minutes loomed, his neck now hurting from the strain of looking up, he finally spied the longed-for movement: a purplish speck slowly parted itself from the tower. Oh joy! Raffi nearly jumped and cheered. The tiny machine sped arrowlike to a safer distance, then began to sink. He could see two figures aboard. So he got her. Thank Bo! Lower they sank, and closer. Just twenty stories to go now. He could even see the blue of Sal's hair. So focused was Raffi on the approaching craft, so excited at the prospect of its imminent arrival, that he failed to notice, at the extreme left of his vision, a blood red arc of flame project itself from one of Time Tower's very lowest balconies. It was like a spout of crimson water, fringed with creamy gold. And it splashed against the side of Dario's bike, sending up a dazzling spray of sparks and stars that reflected in the visors of the riders' helmets. Raffi blinked, half-blinded, and when his vision returned he saw they were on fire. To avoid the leaping flames, Sal had climbed to a precarious standing position on the seat, clutching Dario's shoulders, as he tried to control the wildly veering, dipping, spiralling machine. Down he plunged, much too fast, much too steeply. Then, just as the concourse seemed about to smack him a deathblow in the face, he veered upwards. More dips and twists were followed by another uncontrollable dive, this time almost on his side, like a hover-track racer taking a bend at an insane angle, with Sal somehow holding on behind. The bike hit the ground some twenty metres from Raffi. Sal flew off and bounced, then rolled to a stop. The bike, with Dario still aboard, bumped, skidded and sparked against the tiles for a further thirty metres before finally flopping onto its side.

Raffi sprinted to them. He reached Sal first. Her eyes were closed tight and she had a gash on her leg and blood on her forehead. He whispered to her. 'You okay, Sal?'

He could see the pain in her eyes as she opened them. 'I think so. How's Dario?'

'I'll tell you in a minute. Wait here.'

Raffi found him sitting, forearms resting on his knees, next to the bike. 'Told you I don't die easy,' he grinned. His sweat-shiny face, smeared with soot, reflected the flames from the still-burning machine. 'How's my girl?'

'Knocked for six, but I think she'll be okay.'

'Help me up, would ya, mate?'

'That was some piece of flying just then.'

Dario laughed as he hobbled, with Raffi's support, towards Sal. 'Yeah! And what about that landing!'

He helped Sal to her feet. 'You okay, girl?'

Her affirmative was cut short by a sharp intake of breath as she put weight on her foot. 'Just a sprain, I think – hope!' She looked up at Dario, her hard little face trembling on the verge of laughter or tears, Raffi couldn't tell which. In the end, she just smiled. 'Thanks, Dario!'

'So what took you so long up there?' Raffi asked as he

walked, and they limped, slowly back across the concourse. He didn't wish to confess to his morbid speculations.

'Ah, you know women,' said Dario. 'They say they'll be ready in a minute, but it's always more like ten!'

'You've just lost a large amount of recently won kudos with that remark,' said Sal.

'Seriously,' Raffi wanted to know. 'What happened?'

Dario explained. 'My dear, sweet Mandy – probably the last truly sane MAID in Time Tower – fell off her perch this afternoon. Wrecked the apartment. Sal had to take refuge in the corridor. Took me a while to find her.'

'The whole place has gone mad,' added Sal. 'In the last few hours, while you guys were gone, I've seen some things that I'd love to forget, but probably never will.'

'Such as?'

Sal never managed to say. A black shadow rose up behind her and she fell silently to the ground. Dario began to react, but had managed no more than a quarter turn before he, too, was overwhelmed by the same dark force. Raffi started to run, but was knocked sideways by an impact like a maglev bullet train. His last sensation was of an eye-juddering blow to the head, then the world mercifully winked out.

CHAPTER TEN

RED'S DOMAIN

The human brain is a very great and complex machine, but it's worth nothing if its component parts aren't talking to each other. Within Raffi's semi-concussed head, intercommunication was patchy at best. Although some of the peripheral components were engaged in lively discourse, quite a few of the more fundamental ones were barely on speaking terms. His sensory neurons, for example, were busy flagging up pain to his thalamus long before he recalled how he might go about relieving it. And his olfactory bulb was passing disapproving messages to his cerebrum some while before he remembered how to move his hand to his nose to block the bad smells. Gradually, however, the random electrical impulses that were flashing around his skull began to rediscover their familiar neural pathways, and the exploded jelly of his consciousness began to coalesce.

He blinked.

For a long time that was about as much as he could

manage. Then, hours later, he blinked again, this time more slowly, and his waking brain struggled to make sense of the torrent of visual data that briefly washed down his optic nerve. Flickering shadows? Yellow carpet? Red curtain? That was enough for now. Too much, in fact. The pain in his head would not permit any more. He slept. Again, in his dreams, that odour assaulted his nostrils: a smell of unwashed bodies, smoke and, more faintly, latrines. And he heard sounds: a rumble of voices, a crackle of laughter. For a long time he felt oppressively hot and his hands and feet tried instinctively to throw off blankets that weren't there. Sweat soaked the sheets. Gradually, the heat faded. Water was poured between his lips, and he gratefully swallowed it.

Finally, after a further unmeasurable period, Raffi opened his eyes more fully. His headache now diminished, he forced himself to sit up, so he could see his surroundings more clearly. His bruised ribs complained loudly at the action. He was on a metal-framed hospital-style bed in the middle of a rough-constructed room containing three other, similar beds and nothing else. The floor was of yellowing, dying grass. The 'wall' to his right was a long, rippling, wine-red curtain supported by a pole. The other three sides of the room were composed of sections of lightweight partition walling of the kind usually found in offices and stores. These had been buttressed at regular intervals by angled pieces of timber planted in the soil. On each of the solid walls, a flaming torch had been hung, and the flickering light was reflected in every fold of the curtain. The ceiling was a motley assortment of overlapping corrugated plastic sheets. From the view through a window cut into one of the walls, he saw that he was in a park, with paths and neat squares of shrubs and flowering plants. The plants, he saw, were dying or dead, no longer able to photosynthesise in these dark days, and withered by the desert light and heat that dazzled briefly each day. And what will happen to us, his tired mind wondered, without this vital carbon dioxide sink? Secrocon's decision to switch off the lights would very soon make this world unsustainable for all life. Perhaps that was their plan. From the orange glow of dying fires glimpsed through the thick line of trees, Raffi guessed he was in Solstice Park, territory of Red Oakes and his gang. So it was they who must have jumped him, Dario and Sal.

A movement behind made him turn. One corner of the curtain had been flung aside and a tall, well-muscled biker boy stood there. He wore an open-face helmet. His black poromeric leather unisuit had been augmented by bulky metal armour on his shoulders, arms, legs and crotch area. On his chest was a red wedge shape, curved to look a little like an axe head, with the letters RD crudely inked within. Wordlessly, the boy beckoned. Raffi rose from the bed and followed him. On the other side of the curtain was another room of similar dimension, this one containing a bucket, a bowl for washing and a table and some chairs.

Raffi followed him through a doorway that led outside. In the park, torches fixed to tall wooden posts partially illuminated an industrious scene. He saw approaching lines of armoured, leatherclad men carrying walls, doors, windows and sheets of roofing through the trees towards the central clearing of the park where the buildings were situated. Others, both male and female – though it was hard to tell them apart in their similar clothing – were engaged in erecting walls, hammering in supports, sawing wood and fitting rooves. Smells of sweat, smoke and decay hung heavily in the air. Already ten buildings had been completed, including the one he'd just stepped out of. The progress was impressive. When he'd last looked – was it only yesterday morning? – there had been just one building. The dedication in the faces of the work gangs suggested they really did believe they could create something here. A long line of red, armoured hoverbikes stood near one of the buildings. From a rope strung between the two tallest wooden posts was draped a large sheet daubed with the same red wedge symbol Raffi had seen on his escort's chest.

He was shown into a building positioned at the centre of the settlement. Its walls were higher and looked sturdier than the others, and the roof was pitched. He entered an anteroom with one side curtained off. In front of the curtains stood two huge armoured guards, also wearing biker helmets. Their massive chests bore the same red wedge icon. The sleeves of their leather suits had been ripped away, revealing oil-shiny arms as thick and sinewy as young tree trunks. In their meaty hands each of them supported a shoulder-launched flamethrower, presumably stolen from police androids during the recent battle.

'A guest of our leader,' the escort announced. 'The name's Delgado. He's expecting him.'

The guards stood aside and Raffi was ushered within.

Red Oakes, instantly recognisable in his trademark scarlet leathers, was standing by a torchlit table between two other bikers, looking at a large, sketchily drawn map covered with black crosses and blue marker pen arrows. He continued his murmured conversation with them while Raffi waited. He was short and stocky of build, scarcely taller than Jonah, yet he radiated authority. The battle scar on his cheek helped, making him look older and harder than the posh Island City boy of just a week or so ago. On seeing Raffi, his forehead furrowed and his upper lip curled in undisguised loathing.

'Welcome to my domain, Delgado, old chap,' he whispered through gritted teeth. 'Sorry for the blow to the head. Sorry I didn't deliver it myself if I'm honest. Only if I'd done it, you wouldn't still be breathing.'

'Why do you hate me so much, Rupert?'

Red looked shocked, then angry, at his use of that name. 'Don't try to act familiar with me,' he sneered. 'Don't think our worlds intersect even remotely. I could have you killed like that!' He snapped his fingers. 'The only reason you're still alive is because I can't let you die while you still harbour the illusion that you're better than me. That race... that victory of yours, Delgado, was a fluke. You should never have won it. You're a kid from the outlands, dammit, racing on a bike you hadn't even paid for – racing against an expensively nurtured hybrid of human talent and cutting-edge technology. My father invested millions of u-dolls in me. Millions! He built me into the ultimate racer specifically so I could win the Paridex. I had no other purpose. And it was all going to plan. I could see the light-sword, I could almost taste the victory coolfizz... Until, in those last few seconds, like some freak of nature, you managed to snatch it from me.'

'There's always next year, Red!'

'No! There isn't always next year,' he spat. 'The creditors have caught up with father and he'll probably be in Londaris Penitentiary this time next year. They'll dismantle me and flog my bionic parts to the highest bidder. No, this was my last chance of being champion, and papa will never forgive me for failing him. But, you know, Delgado, I didn't really fail him, did I?' Red's eyes grew wide as he smiled and nodded to himself. 'Because I was the best that day, and you know it. Technically you may have got to the line before me, but I was the better racer. I held back just enough power in reserve to outpace you on the final sprint. I had you well beaten. Your little stunt at the end there with the St Christopher was a trick, a cheat.' He tutted disapprovingly. 'It should never have been allowed.

'Which is why I'm going to prove to you – and everyone here – that I really am the champion. I'm going to race you now, Delgado. Five laps of my domain – Solstice Park. Five laps, just like the Paridex. Are you game, old chap?' He spread his lips and raised his eyebrows challengingly.

'And if I refuse?'

'You die,' he said cheerfully.

'Well then, I'm game, I guess.'

'Excellent! Five times round the course – the way is lit by flamelight. First back to the park gate on the final lap is the winner. Oh, and if you lose, you die. After all, I'm only keeping you alive to prove to you that I'm the better racer. Once that point's been made, there's no further reason not to kill you, is there?'

'And if I win?'

Red laughed long and loud at this. Even his two henchmen and the guards joined in. He shook his head and began moving towards the exit. 'You won't win,' he chuckled. 'See you out there in five minutes.'

CHAPTER ELEVEN

WIN OR DIE

affi sat astride the hoverbike by the park gate. Around sixty leather-jacketed teens stood to either side of the hastily marked track that led round the park. They were laughing and chatting. This was probably the first break they'd had from the non-stop work of building the camp. He scanned the crowd for signs of Dario, Sal, Jonah or Lastara, but couldn't spot them. He hoped they were okay, wherever they were – sad to think he might never see them again. A great cheer went up and the crowd parted as a scarlet-jacketed figure glided up on his big maroon racing bike. Red flashed a grin and gave a short wave. He looked very confident.

Through the gloom ahead, Raffi could see a line of torches heading off in a westerly direction before curving south and out of sight. He had no idea what hazards might lie beyond that point. The first lap would be a journey of discovery. He studied the machine they'd given him. It felt a bit flimsy and lightweight compared to Red's heavyweight racer. That might actually be a good thing if there were trees and things to be negotiated – but on a clear, straight run, you had to bet on Red.

A long-haired, bearded fellow stepped forward holding a flame-torch. 'Okay boys, let's have a fair race,' he sniggered. 'Ignition on.' Raffi pressed the starter button and felt the warm flare of plasma below his feet. He lowered his visor. He'd never felt so nervous before a race, but then the stakes had never been this high. The flame-torch swung downwards, and Raffi twisted hard on the throttle. His bike shot forward, but Red's reflexes were very slightly faster. He moved ahead and was already curving away between the line of flame-torches while Raffi sped along in his wake. Raffi usually prided himself on his good starts – he liked to dominate races from the beginning. Perhaps the blow to his head had affected his reactions, or perhaps Dookie Oakes's engineers had tuned up Red's to lightning speed. Either way, Raffi was now in the unfamiliar role of playing catch-up. The western side of the wedge-shaped park was open, flat, treeless and downhill, allowing Red to extend his lead dramatically. Soon he was a maroon dot in the distance. Raffi could do no more than keep his head down and his throttle open, and hope for more promising terrain ahead. As he turned into the southern bend, he got his wish. The trees were parched and leafless from the long nights and short, fiercely hot days, but they still provided a challenge, especially for a big bike like Red's.

By the time the two of them had picked their way through the forest and began heading up the east side, the gap between them had become appreciably smaller. To Raffi's right were the smouldering ruins on Solstice Avenue and, halfway up, both bikes had to swerve left then right to circumnavigate part of Solstice Square. He noticed that Red was being cautious on the bends, taking them relatively wide and slow, confident that he could always make up the time on the straights – there may be some profit to be made on the bends, thought Raffi. As they started to turn west on the final stretch of the first lap, he took it very fast, applying a minimum of air brake, and when they whizzed past the finish-line crowds at the park gate, there was no more than fifteen metres between them. Red restored the big gap once more on the long, flat west side, but Raffi, familiar now with the track, more than made up for this through the southern forest, the next two bends and the swerve around Solstice Square.

As they completed the second lap, Raffi was just ten metres to the rear. He tried the same tactic on Lap Three, taking the turns as fast as he could manage, almost recklessly in fact – whether he crashed out or lost, death awaited him, so why play safe? By the end of the lap he had closed the gap to five metres. On Lap Four he threw himself into the bends with ever more careless abandon, knowing time was starting to run out on him. The tree branches whistled desperately close to his right elbow and knee as he danced through the southern forest. By the time he flung himself into the final bend, they were neck and neck, and – to the disappointed gasps of the partisan finish-line crowd – Raffi was slightly ahead as they completed the fourth lap. The tension and anxiety were evident in their watching faces. They had all expected this to be an easy stroll, a victory procession for their leader, their champion. And so, surely, had Red. What could he be thinking now? 'His mistake', thought Raffi jubilantly, 'was to give me too much motivation. When defeat means death, I've got nothing to lose!' Raffi's smile was nearly wiped permanently off his face just then as his prow hit the dirt on the north-west bend, sending up sparks and almost tipping him over. With supreme skill, and not a small amount of strength, he managed to right the machine and send it back on its way. 'Careful now, boy,' he chided himself. 'You're not home yet.' The trouble was that his chosen tactic – his only possible tactic – relied on almost superhuman levels of concentration at every bend. Now, thanks to that stupid error, he'd let Red back into the race.

As they roared down the west-side downhill straight on the final lap, he felt the boy breathing down his neck and was then forced to watch helplessly as Red retook the lead. In an almost suicidally reckless manoeuvre, Raffi cut inside him on the south-west bend, and as they entered the forest they were inseparable. Raffi knew he only had to keep concentrating now to win. His bike was more manoeuvrable than Red's and from here on in it was all about who was better on the bends. A glance to his left told him that Red knew this, too. The boy's mouth and cheeks were contorted with rage and hate. Then, out of the corner of his eye, Raffi saw Red's bike make a small yet sudden leftward swerve, right into his path. Raffi tried to swerve himself to get out of the way, but was unable to avoid a minor collision. Sparks flew as Red's prow struck Raffi's rear fender. Raffi's bike wobbled, but he managed to rebalance himself just in time to avoid hitting a tree. To his amazement, Red then came at him again, striking him hard at the skirt-like base of the bike, near the port-side propulsor. Part of the prow caught Raffi's calf, sending hot, jagged pain shooting through his leg. Raffi's bike was now seriously unbalanced. As he wobbled about, he glimpsed Red's grin, and he suddenly understood his game: under cover of the forest, no one would be able to see him force his opponent into a crash.

Raffi, now flying in a chaotic, barely controlled slalom, felt the tips of the branches brushing his helmet and slicing into his exposed cheek. Then Red came for him a third time, clearly intending to finish him off by nudging him into the denser forest to the left of the path. But Raffi, reading Red's intentions, swiftly applied his air brakes. Red sailed on, unable to pull out of his swerve in time, and his bike smashed hard into a tree, bursting into flames. Raffi brought his bike down on the path and limped as fast as he could back to the burning wreckage. The heat was intense and it was hard to see through the smoke, but he saw Red engulfed in the fire. Without thinking, Raffi reached into the inferno, grabbed hold of Red's jacket and pulled him clear. His visor and gloves provided some protection from the red-hot sparks, but it felt like a blast furnace on his scratched and bleeding face. He used his own jacket to douse the flames that were burning the boy's clothes and skin. Others began arriving now, having witnessed the fireball in the forest from their vantage point on the park's northern rise. Someone used water to extinguish the remaining flames on Red's jacket while the gang's medic came forward to tend his wounds.

CHAPTER TWELVE

THE REAL RUPERT OAKES

The next few hours were anxious and confusing ones for the inhabitants of Red's Domain. The gangsters huddled in small groups, talking quietly and waiting for news from the medical hut about their leader. Raffi sat on a stool outside his dormitory while a gum-chewing biker girl with red streaks in her hair dressed the wound on his thigh. The only light she had was a small, flickery torch attached to the wall above their heads.

Three male bikers approached, including the bearded one who'd started the race. 'Hey, stranger, you gonna tell us what occurred in the forest, then?' said beardy. From his fierce look, he clearly thought Raffi had indulged in some foul play.

Raffi knew they wouldn't believe the truth, so he just shrugged and replied: 'Nothing. It was an accident, that's all.'

'Yeah, like 'ell it was!' sneered another of them, a tall young man with a bald head that gleamed in the torchlight.

He grabbed Raffi's collar and lifted him clear off the stool. 'P'raps you'd like to tell us what really 'appened, racer-boy.'

'Hey, leave it out, Skull,' said the girl who'd been tending Raffi. 'The boy jus' told you, din't 'e? Said it was an accident, right? When Red's back on 'is feet, we'll 'ear all about it. So let's not be too hasty in judgin' the boy till then, awright?'

Skull emitted a snarl through his bared teeth as his eyes bored into Raffi's. Then he opened his fist, causing Raffi to drop painfully back onto the stool.

The men retreated, and Raffi thanked the girl for her intervention.

'I don' know you,' she replied. 'All I know is that you was brave out there on the track. You raced without fear. An' I don' think anyone who races like that would cheat. There now.' She sat back. 'That's the best I can manage. I'll 'ave to leave you to it now. Okay, stranger?'

'Thanks again,' said Raffi. The girl smiled at him then sauntered back to her friends.

Raffi checked out the neat white bandage. He started to get up. But the sight that greeted him just then made him rock back down on the stool. Out of the gloom emerged Dario, Jonah and Sal. They were walking up the short rise towards him.

'Hey, mate!' Dario clasped Raffi's outstretched palm, and Jonah embraced him. Sal, as ever, held back, offering no more than a tight-lipped smile.

'We heard about your heroics in the race,' smiled Dario. 'Sounds like you gave Red a good run for his money.'

'Where were you?'

'They were holding us under guard in a hut further down the hill,' said Jonah. 'But in all the confusion after the race, we managed to get out.' He surveyed the subdued throngs of gangsters scattered around the park. 'No one seems particularly bothered that we've escaped. I think they're all feeling a bit directionless at the moment.'

'Where's Lastara?'

Jonah looked bleak at the mention of her name.

'We don't know where she is,' said Sal.

'We were just sitting there waiting for you guys,' said Jonah, 'when some of Red's crew attacked us. I was knocked out and woke up here. I've been asking people where she is, but they swear they've no idea. They said I was on my own when they attacked. I've been going over and over it in my head and I'm sure she was there with me.'

'Don't be too downhearted, Jonah,' said Raffi. 'Maybe that mysterious friend of hers popped up and rescued her at the last minute.'

The heavily muscled biker boy who had escorted him to Red earlier that day now reappeared before them. Ignoring the others, he addressed Raffi. 'Our leader would like to see you. Please come this way.'

Raffi glanced at his friends. Jonah looked anxious, but Dario pursed his lips in an encouraging smile, and patted him on the back. Then Raffi hobbled off through the shadows after the biker.

The interior of the medical hut was kept purposefully dim, with the only light coming from torches glimmering in the park beyond the windows. 'Is that you, Delgado?' came a hoarse whisper from a corner of the room, screened off by curtains.

'Yes.'

'Come in, old chap. Come and see what's left of me.'

Hesitantly, Raffi pulled back the curtain. A medic was seated by the bedside, brushing anti-burn solution onto Red's forearm. Raffi's eyes were getting used to the dark by now, and he could discern Red's heavily bandaged figure, and the terrible scarring all over the bottom half of his face where the helmet hadn't shielded him from the blaze. His chin and cheeks were swollen and shiny pink and his mouth was a lipless slit through which Raffi could see his moist tongue restlessly moving.

With a wave of his bandaged hand, Red signalled for the medic to leave them.

'I wish you'd left me to burn, Delgado,' he sighed bitterly once they were alone. 'Look at me. What's the point of me now?' Scarcely able to move his lips, his words were mumbled and hard to understand. The smoke damage to his lungs gave his voice a rasping, rattling sound.

'There are people out there waiting and hoping for your recovery,' answered Raffi. 'They need the confidence and leadership you can give them. That's the point of you.'

'I don't think I can give them that any more,' he mumbled softly into his pillow. 'All my life it was drummed into me that I was the best, the champion-in-waiting. That belief made me what I am – what I was. But I don't feel that way now. You and I know I'm not that – far from it. So where does that leave me, Delgado? What's left of me now I know I'm not the best – now I know I'm just a loser and a cheat and a – a fraud?' This speech trailed off into a harsh coughing fit.

'I can't answer that, Red. Except that I think there's more to you than the… creature your dad tried to turn you into. You should turn your back on that. You should try and find the real Rupert Oakes beneath the layers of machinery and implants–'

Red raised his bandaged hand as if to say he'd heard enough. Raffi noticed that a tear had welled in a dip at the top of one of his cheeks. 'I'm so sorry, Raffi,' he wept. 'I'm sorry for hating you and for wanting to kill you. Go now, will you. My deputy Lars Nyman will take command for now. He'll brief you on our situation. I hope you'll see fit to join us.'

Raffi turned to leave, but as he stepped through the curtain, he heard Red cry out. 'Why, Raffi?'

'Why what?' asked Raffi, turning.

'Why did you pull me from those flames? Why?!'

Raffi thought for a moment. 'There was no why about it, Red. I saw someone in trouble, and I acted.'

CHAPTER THIRTEEN

No More Secrets, No More Tomorrows

alf an hour later, Raffi, Dario, Sal and Jonah were summoned for a meeting in the war room with Lars Nyman. He was a big, tough, no-nonsense fellow – in a former life he'd been a gang leader in one of the poorer outland settlements. He looked at each of them before speaking. 'I'm sorry for the way we nabbed yer in Time Tower an' on the concourse. We din't 'ave much time. We 'ad to do it for yer own protection. The situation has changed in the last 24 hours. In fact it's changin' by the hour. As things stand there's no place for individuals or small groups around 'ere. Time Tower is quickly turning into a shitpit of the first order. The Lower Tower mob, once they've wiped out everyone above Floor 100 and found nothin' worth stealin', are goin' to start streamin' out the bottom of the tower like 'ungry dogs on the prowl, an' you lot would a been dogfood in a matter of minutes. That's why we brought you 'ere.'

'Can't you guys do something about the wholesale

slaughter going on in the Upper Tower?' asked Raffi. 'Can't you launch some kind of rescue – to at least get the remaining people out of there before they're killed?'

Lars looked at him, his steel-grey eyes dancing as he considered the question. 'Red an' I thought about it, but nah... We saw what 'appened to Dario. Nearly lost 'is life twice up there. We can't afford to lose any of our men on a mad, doomed mission. We've got other priorities. Come 'ere an' I'll show you.' He pointed to a map on a torchlit table.

The map Lars pointed to showed a plan of the entire Topside, with Time Tower at the centre and the avenues radiating outwards from it like spokes on a wheel. Between each spoke were green wedge shapes depicting parks, gardens and wilder areas. He pointed to one green wedge on the southern side of the wheel. 'This is Solstice Park, Red's Domain. After some 'ard battles with neighbourin' tribes, our forces now control the two borderin' avenues, Solstice and Tomorrow, the streets linkin' em, and all their stores an' eathouses. We got generators runnin' again in all these places, so we can freeze and refrigerate food. Basically, we can feed our 100 or so followers quite 'appily for the next couple a months. Food ain't the problem. The problem is that we're still too small, which makes us vulnerable to attack from larger tribes to the north and east. To survive, we 'ave ter expand.'

He pointed to the region north-west of Solstice. 'This way is Tomorrow Fields, Interim, Calendar. We could easily take 'em, but there ain't too much food over there. Occupyin' the area would stretch our forces for little gain. The north 'ere is controlled by Stimson Grebe's gang, now run by a bird they call Austra Bella – and we're not going to mess with them. Nah, the obvious thing is to aim north-east: Transient Ridge, Periodic Park, Lake Perpetuity. That's where the rich pickin's are, and from what I've 'eard, not well defended by

Potter Logan's crew. But we have ter strike before Austra Bella, who must be thinkin' the same thing.'

Raffi was tempted to point out the many flaws in Lars' plan: the fact that Secrocon could destroy them in an instant simply by turning the lights on; the fact that everyone would probably start suffocating in a few weeks anyway, when there was no more plantlife to absorb the carbon dioxide that everyone was breathing out. The whole Sphere was going rapidly to hell, and none of Lars' expansion plans would change that inescapable fact.

He might well have said something along these lines, but was unable to because at that moment the curtain swished back and a soldier entered. 'Sir, enemy hoverbikes spotted in formation to the east over Hawking Hills. Possible attack imminent.'

'Potter Logan's mob,' growled Lars. 'They musta known we'd be comin' for 'em.' He gave a lopsided grin. 'Send up Three and Four Squadrons,' he ordered. 'Take–'

But before Lars could complete the instruction, he was interrupted by a burst of energy projectiles outside the hut. The soldier's knees buckled and he began falling forwards, then froze, flickering like a faulty lightbulb for a second or two before disappearing. A hooded gunman charged into the hut, spraying bolts of laser energy as he went. Everyone, including Raffi, ran for what limited cover they could find behind chairs and tables, but Sal was too late. Raffi saw three or four projectiles slam into her back, their force sending her flying. Her splayed body hung motionless in the air, flickering as the soldier's had done – then Sal was no more. Dario was next to disappear, and, seconds later, Lars. At the same time, Raffi felt a scorching pain in his leg that put the earlier injury to shame. His eyesight began to blur and the world started flying away from him in at least four contradictory directions.

Then the scene his eyes were showing him changed. Lars was still calmly describing his plan. The others – Sal, Dario, Jonah – were standing by the map table just as they had been a minute before. The knife-like pain in his leg was gone.

The curtain swished back and the soldier entered, just as before. 'Sir, enemy hoverbikes spotted in formation to the east over Hawking Hills. Possible attack imminent.'

A rezzy flash! Raffi had been suffering these ever since his spell on the Underside. The technicians at the Re-Ed Centre had put him inside a desynchronisation machine that had sent him a few minutes into the past. Then Septimus Watts rescued him and Dario and used another machine to resynchronise them. But Raffi's resynchronisation had been slightly botched, leaving him with these occasional, brief glimpses of the imminent future.

'Quick!' cried Raffi, before Lars could say anything. 'There's going to be an attack on this hut in the next minute. A man on his own. He's got some kind of crazy gun – like a dilator but it makes people disappear.'

'What're you talkin' about?' demanded Lars.

'He's always right about these things, Lars,' said Dario. 'Trust me!'

Lars shrugged. 'Okay, Ganeri. You 'eard the boy. Get out there and keep yer eyes peeled.

'Very good, sir.'

Thirty seconds later, they heard a loud thud. The hooded man Raffi had seen earlier was brought in – dead. Lars inspected the insignia on the dark blue hood. 'One o' Logan's special operatives,' he murmured. 'Decapitation strike. They prob'ly thought I was Red. Killing the leader would've made the invasion so much easier. I 'ave to thank you Raffi for that timely prediction of yours.' He extracted the weapon from the man's holster and examined it. 'Says Temp Fi-Er. I ain't never seen one o' these before.'

'Temp Fi-Er stands for temporal field eraser,' said Jonah. 'They delete people in time as well as space. Once hit by one of those, you're not only dead – it's as if you never lived. I suspect it's a battle trophy from their fight with the Secrocon police.'

Jonah's words stirred a vague memory in Raffi. He felt he'd been confronted by one of these guns before, but couldn't say exactly when or where.

Lars grunted and pocketed the gun. 'Okay Ganeri, now let's deal with the rest of 'em.'

The soldier saluted, and was gone. Lars turned back to the others. 'I need good people – engineers, as well as soldiers.' He looked at Raffi. 'I need talents like the one you've just shown most of all... If you people wanna survive in the new, lawless Chronosphere, you could do worse than join us. What d'ya say? Will you join our tribe?' Surveying their uncertain faces, he said: 'Okay then, sleep on it. I'll want your answer by the morning.'

⧗

As they left the war room, 14 or 15 bikes were rising into the dark sky, bound for Hawking Hills. Dario and Jonah walked ahead, while Raffi walked with Sal. She touched his arm.

'What is it?' he asked.

Sal's small mouth was taut with worry. She looked a mess – her cropped blue hair as matted and unwashed as an old rug, and there were dark insomnia crescents under her eyes. 'We haven't got long to live, have we, Raffi?' She looked around her, at the dead and dying vegetation. He could see she'd reached the same conclusion as he had. 'Lars talked about expanding his tinpot empire this way and that, but it's pointless because in a few weeks we'll all be dead – I know you think so, too. I could see it from your expression in there.'

Raffi nodded.

'You're the only one who knows the real reason I'm here,' she said softly, glancing over her shoulder. 'I've spent a year scouring the place for Anna. I've been through records at the Info Centre, I've knocked on domicile doors throughout Time Tower with her photo, but I've got nowhere. And now I'm having to face the fact that I might die without ever seeing her again, without ever knowing whether she even survived.' She nodded towards the hulking sillhouette of Time Tower to the north. 'There's just one little theory that I keep coming back to. Remember that conversation we had, about six months ago, when you said you'd seen all those teenagers down in the Re-Education Centre? I keep thinking… could it be… do you think it's possible… that they made an exception for Anna? I know she was 23, but–'

'No!' said Raffi emphatically, but he couldn't help a sigh of anguish escaping. The longer he'd kept his secret from her, the harder it had become to tell her, and the heavier the burden of guilt.

Seven months earlier, while he was on the Underside, trying to escape the security guards in the Re-Ed Centre, Raffi had come upon a beautiful girl held in solitary confinement. Her name was Anna and she was living her life in reverse. Before he was captured, he'd vowed to come back for her. For a while he'd been quite obsessed by her. When Sal later told him about her sister, also called Anna, he strongly suspected that the two were the same, and that they were time-reversng Anna back to teenagehood. But by then his thoughts were on leaving the Sphere. The last thing he'd wanted was to be dragged back into another adventure on the Underside. If he'd told Sal about Anna, then she would most definitely have wanted to go and rescue her, and she would have needed Raffi to guide her there. The chances were they'd have been captured and tortured and time-shifted to some remote place in the distant past, never to be seen or heard of again. Raffi couldn't bear that idea, so he mentally abandoned Anna to her fate, and said nothing to Sal.

He never completely forgot about her. A few times since then he'd promised himself that he'd talk to Sal about Anna, and each time it was easier to put it off until the next day. I'll tell her tomorrow, he told himself. But the way things were going, soon there would be no more tomorrows – and, with such little time left, there shouldn't be any more secrets, not between friends. He lowered his head. 'I mean yes,' he said very quietly. 'You're right. I think she's down there in the Re-Ed Centre. I think I met your sister while I was down there. I'm almost sure it was her.'

Sal stared at him, her eyes like fire – or was it ice? – the look burned in any case. From nearby came raucous singing from a bunch of bikers, which only served to intensify Sal's deadly silence.

'Tell me what you know,' she demanded, her eagerness for information for the moment trumping her anger, though the anger would surely follow.

Raffi told her about his encounter in the cell, the fact she'd been time-reversed, and his theory that they were taking her back into teenagehood.

Sal's hands went to her mouth when he described her physical appearance. 'That's her,' she groaned, and tears started from her eyes. 'Did she… did she seem… lonely?'

He nodded.

Sal wiped her eyes with the back of her hand. 'We must go to her. Get her out of there.'

Raffi had anticipated this. He guessed that conditions down below were probably even worse than they were Topside, and he rated the chances of a successful rescue at somewhere close to zero. And even if they found her, any reunion was bound to be very brief. Yet, despite this, he didn't hesitate. 'Yes,' he said. 'I want to help. I feel terrible, Sal, for not telling you before.'

'Why? Why didn't you?' She seemed more puzzled than angry. She probably assumed he had a good reason.

Raffi knew his next words would make him despicable in her eyes, but he said them anyway. 'Fear,' he said. 'And selfishness. I knew you'd need me to guide you there, and I knew the chances were we'd be caught. I didn't want to face that possibility, not after what I'd seen down there – the torture, the–'

'You could have just told me. I wouldn't have made you go with me.'

Raffi turned away, towards the trees, unable to cope any longer with her ice-hot stare. 'Yeah, but I would have felt obliged to. And I would have felt like a coward for saying no. I didn't want that.' He turned back to her. 'Look, I've been the worst kind of idiot. But I want to make it up to you, Sal, in any way I can. I want to help you find Anna.'

Sal took a deep breath and lowered her eyelids, as if searching for some inner calm. 'Okay,' she said. 'I'm going to try very hard not to go crazy now. I'm going to try not to think about all the months we've wasted with my sister rotting away down there. I'm going to try to be practical and suppress any violent urges I might have towards you, at least for now... If they time-reversed her three and a half years ago, she'll be very nearly 19 by now. We may be too late. Whatever it is they do to teenagers down there, they may already be doing it to Anna. We've got no time to waste: we have to go now. Tonight. Do you know how to get down there?'

He nodded. 'There's a shaft underneath Parsim Pennyminder's Cosmetic Enhancement Store on Fleeting Avenue. But Sal, it'll be suicide to try to get there on our own. We need help. Maybe Lars can lend us an escort.'

Sal bit her lip, fighting more reckless impulses. 'Okay,' she said after a minute. 'We'll ask him. But I'm going tomorrow, whether he decides to help us or not.'

When they returned to their barracks, they found Jonah and Dario at the table playing cards.

'So where've you two been then?' asked Dario.

Raffi looked at Sal, who nodded her assent. The boys listened boggle-eyed and frequently open-mouthed as Raffi explained Sal's secret mission, his encounter with Anna, and their decision to try and rescue her.

'But you saw her months ago, mate? Why only mention this now.'

'Let's just say I've been a fool.'

Dario simply shrugged. His best and worst quality was that he never judged a friend. 'I'm sure you had your reasons,' he said. 'But no matter. A rescue attempt would be crazy. You've got to hike across hostile territory just to get to the shaft. And we've no idea what conditions are like on the Underside. If it's bad up here, it's probably ten times worse down there.' He frowned. 'It's an insane and foolhardy mission, and almost certainly doomed. But you two can't do it alone. Count me in.'

'And me,' shrugged Jonah. 'After all,' he added wistfully, 'What have I got to live for here?'

CHAPTER FOURTEEN

⏳

THE SUICIDE SQUAD

The next morning, Sal awoke Dario and Raffi early. The three of them got dressed, then asked the guard posted outside the barrackroom for an audience with Lars. An hour went by – most frustrating for Sal, who was the keenest to be gone – before they were admitted to the war room.

Lars's reply was instant and categorical. 'You gotta be jokin'. No way on earth am I goin' to risk my men and machines on a shit-fer-brains scheme like that. You'd be crossin' right through Logan and Bella's airspace. It'd be shootin' practice for over a hundred snipers. I'd be amazed if you got 'alf a kilometre. If you lot are so keen on killin' yerselves, you'll 'ave to do it alone.'

Sal, who had perhaps anticipated this response, now spoke up. 'You said yesterday you wanted to attack Potter Logan, right?'

Lars frowned. 'What about it?'

'Well, the best way of achieving surprise would be to create some kind of diversion.'

'What're you goin' on about?'

'We could be that diversion.' She moved over to the wall map, and the men instinctively followed her. 'I agree with you that four bikes would be suicidal,' said Sal. 'But what about if you sent a whole squadron, even two, in this direction.' She made a sweeping movement with her finger from Solstice Park around Time Tower and across to Fleeting Avenue. 'Logan would assume you were attacking him from the north, and he'd send his forces to meet the threat. You could then send your entire remaining force on a full frontal assault to the east.'

Lars looked at the map for a long time without speaking. He rubbed his chin. 'A diversion,' he muttered. Then he turned to a guard. 'Call McKenzie and Quinn.'

A moment later, the two men Raffi had seen with Red the day before entered. Lars introduced them as his chief strategists. He demonstrated Sal's idea to them. They were both impressed. 'After his attempted strike last night, Logan knows we'll be hitting back,' said Quinn, 'He's going to be very jumpy today, so he's bound to take the bait.'

'If we move fast,' added McKenzie, 'we'd be able to establish a bridgehead on Transient Avenue before he could get his bikes back from Fleeting.'

'Better still,' said Sal. 'You could try taking Hawking Hills and Transient Ridge. Then you'll have the high ground. From there you could launch an attack on Periodic Park.'

'Madness,' scoffed McKenzie. 'Those hills are too well defended.'

'Nah, she's right,' said Lars. 'We gotta be bold, cos time ain't on our side. When Bella sees us comin' for Logan's Domain, she's gonna try an' steal it out from under us before we even get ourselves dug in. That's why we gotta move fast.

As the girl says, we gotta try an' take the 'igh ground in a single move. An' if this diversion works, those 'ills'll be ripe for the takin'. Now… 'ow soon can we get goin'?'

'I suggest we leave after sundown,' said Quinn. 'We don't want to be exposed on those hills during the midday heat. We can be ready to leave by 14.30.'

'OK, let's do it. We'll use fourteen bikes for the diversionary attack. If we use any less, it won't look real. Make sure they're ready to leave at 14.30. Four of 'em will have to take this crew pillion. They should head north-east, keepin' as close to Time Tower as safety allows. Drop this lot near Fleetin', then start attackin' Logan's forces in Periodic Park. It's a bit of a suicide run, so it's volunteers only: lads without lasses; lasses without lads. The last thing we want is weepin' widders bringin' down the mood o' the camp when their better 'alves don't come back.'

'When should the main strike force head out?' asked McKenzie.

'15.00 hours. Six squadrons – forty-two bikes – in an all-out assault on Hawkin' Hills and Transient Ridge. That'll leave fourteen bikers and a ground force of forty to defend the Home Domain. Any questions?'

McKenzie and Quinn had none.

'Right then. Go tell the guys, and ready the bikes and weapons.'

At noon came the dreaded heat, to be faced this time without the shield of air-conditioning. Red's troop had commandeered some refrigerants and humidifiers from the stores and public buildings along Eternity Avenue, and they placed these in each of the barrack huts to make the conditions more bearable. The four friends stripped down to their underwear and lay on their beds. Despite this, when daybreak came, Raffi still felt like he'd been swaddled in multiple layers of clothing and then smothered by duvets. No one spoke for the next two hours. They barely moved except to drink from their water bottles or wipe the sweat from their bodies. At around 14.00, the room began to darken and breathing became a little easier. Ten minutes later, they got up, washed and put their clothes on.

The Suicide Squad, as the diversionary party, with grim humour, referred to themselves, were lying on the dead grass by their machines waiting for the off. Nine boys and five girls had been chosen from the twenty who'd volunteered. They all struck Raffi as tough kids, similar to those he'd seen in the streets of the poorer outland settlements near where he'd grown up. It wasn't just toughness, though. In their easy yet harsh-sounding laughter he discerned a devil-may-care nonchalance. Unlike Red's inner circle, it wasn't loyalty to their leader that drove these kids, but an addiction to danger – to the thrill of a life lived on the edge.

Dario, Raffi, Jonah and Sal approached the group.

'You guys must be the ones we're droppin' on Fleetin', right?' said a gum-chewing girl with red streaks in her hair. Raffi recognized her as the one who'd tended his wound earlier.

'That's us,' said Dario, sounding a little nervous.

The girl eyed him more closely from her supine position. 'Shame to see a fit lad like you dyin' so cheap.'

'Why don't you give him one,' chuckled another female next to her. 'There's time for a quickie.'

Laughter rippled through the group.

'I'm tempted,' said the first girl. 'Fancy it, darlin'?'

'OK, pipe down Milla,' said a male colleague, who looked to be in charge. 'Now which of you lot has been detailed to take our friends here?'

Four hands went up, including Milla's.

'Right, Baz, you take the big guy; Milla, you take the tall one; Scram, you take the little one; and Skull, you take the girl.'

'But Bowden, can't I take the big guy?' pleaded Milla.

'No. Now are there any further questions? Right, mount up!'

The bikers took their time getting up, stretching, fiddling with their jackets, their weapons, their helmets, chuckling at the odd feeble joke. It was probable that few, perhaps none, would return from this mission, and despite the smiles on their faces, there was a noticeable tension in the set of their shoulders and the way they didn't meet each other's eyes.

Raffi squeezed his helmet onto his head and climbed onto the seat behind Milla, who turned and gave him a wink. 'I know you,' she smiled. 'You're the boy racer, aren't ya?' A strand of red hair had fallen across her forehead. She had a large black gun in a holster strapped to her leatherclad thigh that Raffi couldn't help but find quite sexy.

There was a rapid series of short coughs as fourteen starter motors charged fourteen corona wires, and the bikes rose up on their purple cushions. 'If we come under attack before Fleetin', all bets are off,' she warned him. 'We'll just have to drop ya where we can.'

'Understood,' said Raffi. 'Don't take any extra risks for our sakes.'

Bowden raised his hand, and one by one, the bikes took flight. Raffi looked down on the torchlit encampment known as Red's Domain – twelve-going-on-thirteen plastic-roofed dwellings – a tiny, ugly patch of human life stubbornly clinging on in a dying land. Sitting alone in the mud-churned midst of it, Raffi spotted Red Oakes, who must have wheeled himself out of the medical hut in time to watch the Suicide Squad fly away.

CHAPTER FIFTEEN

WE DID GOOD, DIN'T WE, RACER BOY?

They flew north in an arrowhead formation, with Milla and Raffi on the righthand wing, fourth bike out from the tip. The other bikers were mere shadows above their purple pillows of plasma and Raffi soon gave up trying to pick out his friends. Beneath were the ruined streets between Solstice and Tomorrow, now firmly under Red's control. The only lights were from the torches of the occasional patrol or pillaging unit. Ahead loomed the hulk of Time Tower: once the great hourglass silhouette had represented home; now, knowing the horrors that had taken place within, its shape appeared far more sinister, and Raffi was relieved when the formation began to veer eastwards in a wide arc that kept them well clear of it. They drifted over the old shopping district between Solstice and Eternity, a no-man's land well plundered by Red's troop but not as yet claimed by any gang. On Eternity, Raffi could see the white glowing bubble of the old sports complex-come-hospital. He dreaded to think what conditions were like down there by now.

The bikes climbed higher as they crossed into the Transient-Eternity Sector, Potter Logan's territory. From here on things became markedly more dangerous. Bowden navigated a careful course. If he strayed too close to Time Tower, they would be vulnerable to snipers on the balconies there. If they drifted too far the other way, out over Transient Gardens, Logan's ack-ack batteries would be lying in wait. Altitude was also a balancing act. He didn't want to make it easy for them. On the other hand, the Squad was supposed to act as bait to draw Logan's forces, so they had to be visible. They plateaued at a height just above the waist of Time Tower.

The plan seemed to work. Tens of tiny purple ovals, like little gas flame lighters, began sparking to life in Transient Gardens and up on the Ridge. Logan's forces were on the move. Raffi saw that one group was ascending, heading straight towards them, while the majority were flying just above ground level, towards Periodic Park, to meet a suspected attack from the north. So far, Sal's diversionary ploy was working perfectly. The intercept party was closing in frighteningly fast. Already Raffi could see the gleam on their helmet visors. Bowden gave a signal and the Suicide Squad separated to make themselves a trickier target. Milla tipped her machine hard to the right and downwards, so she and Raffi headed straight into the approaching enemy formation. Raffi clung to her jacket as the sudden extra momentum threatened to unseat him. With her left hand she unclipped a long metal bar from just below her seat. She slid it out from beneath her leg and handed it to Raffi without looking back. He understood that this was to be his weapon. Oh hell! That would mean he would have to let go of her with at least one hand. He swallowed and grabbed it with his right, holding it up at a 45-degree angle from the bike, ready to strike out at any passing machine, while clinging on desperately with his left. Meanwhile, Milla unholstered her

gun and took aim at the nearest biker, who was now just 20
or 30 metres away. A stream of laser energy shot out from the
gun and the enemy bike exploded in a burst of expanding
plasma.

Immediately, they were attacked from the left by another
bike, armed with a flamethrower. The liquid fire, like a
writhing scarlet serpent, dipped just beneath them, causing
the bike to rock violently and sending a wave of heat through
the soles of Raffi's shoes. The black-helmeted rider was
quickly upon them, attempting to seize the advantage while
Milla was still trying to rebalance her machine. He came at
her with a lance. Milla, struggling to control her bike, had no
means of evading the attack. Raffi raised his own weapon
and, with careful timing, brought it down hard on the other
man's wrist. He heard a scream, and the lance tumbled
towards the ground far below.

All around them, against the deep blue backdrop, the air
was suddenly full of dogfights. Logan's black machines
swirled through and around the Squad's claret-hued bikes
like locusts. Bikes wheeled and dodged, jousting with lances,
clashing prow against wing, wing against tail, spewing flames
and sparks, screeching as their metal frames were ripped
apart. Riders, unseated, fell with startled cries towards the
distant parkland. Dense jets of fire arced like deadly hose
spray. Bikes and riders ignited with the quiet thud of inflated
paperbags to become solid ovals of flame and black smoke
that spiralled down, or simply plummeted, very soon just
miniature gold and black specks against the dusky olive
landscape. These sights and sounds struck too quickly for
Raffi to absorb or reflect on. That would come later, although
'later' itself seemed an unlikely notion with death
whisperingly close at every turn. Right now, every nerve
ending in his body was strained to the task of survival. He
was Milla's eyes and ears, screaming at her to bank left or

right to avoid a fire spray or flying lance. His right arm ached from his own heavy weapon, which he swung at any passing enemy bike, though he only rarely managed to connect. Milla was more successful with her gun, zapping two more enemy bikes with direct hits. For the seven or eight minutes of engagement, Raffi saw nothing but what was in front of him. It was only when the smoke finally cleared, and the black bikes, or the few that remained, began wheeling away in hasty retreat that he understood the battle was over and they had won! The surge of relief and elation made him shiver. But his smile quickly faded as he recalled Dario, Jonah and Sal. He counted ten maroon bikes – though he couldn't tell at this stage if they included the mounts carrying his friends. Two bikes were in trouble, moving jerkily with their corona discharges flickering and fading. Bowden's bulky figure, just discernible above them, signalled with raised hand, and the bikes reformed into their arrowhead and continued north towards Spell Street and, distantly visible now, the pale arm of Fleeting Avenue.

They made a gradual descent towards Fleeting, keeping a careful eye on the ranks of black bikes now gathered in Periodic Park. There had to be fifty – near enough Logan's entire airforce. The diversion had worked almost too well: they were heading into a slaughter-ground. And yet a worm of doubt must surely have entered Logan's mind by now: if this was the advance party, where were the rest of Red's forces?

As they passed over Spell Street and headed in for a landing on the far side of a deserted Fleeting Avenue, the bikes of another enemy squadron came to purple life and began sailing up to meet them. This was tentative by Logan. He could have crushed them with even two squadrons, but he must be beginning to smell a rat, with some squadrons now rising and wheeling to return south. Too late, certainly, with Red's main assault group already enroute to Hawking Hills.

While the Squad hovered in attack formation, Milla descended with another bike to the rubble-strewn surface of Fleeting Avenue. Raffi saw Sal's scrawny figure leap from the other bike and immediately take cover in the ruins of what looked like the old Info Centre. The bikes carrying Dario and Jonah were nowhere to be seen.

'Good luck, racer-boy,' shouted Milla, as Raffi dismounted. He saw the respect in her eyes, and hoped she saw something similar in his. As she throttled upwards to rejoin her comrades, he desperately scanned the sky for Dario and Jonah's bikes. Instead he witnessed the arrival of the enemy squadron and its immediate engagement with Bowden's troop, hovering just twenty metres above the ground. It was a fearful assault. Ropes of fire swung and twisted through the air, striking three maroon bikes, brightening the sky with the subsequent explosions. One bike vaporised, and the other two, charred wrecks bearing corpse riders, plunged downwards, one catching Milla as she ascended, and sending her into a tailspin. Raffi watched, shocked and dismayed, as girl and machine crashed to the street behind a mound of rubble. He immediately charged up the hill of blocks and girders and tumbled towards the flaming bike, which had landed halfway down the other side of the mound. He tried to free her from the wreckage, but something metallic dragged as he pulled, something stuck to her, though he couldn't see what it was in the shadows and smoke. Milla gave a gurgled cry of pain. Her lower lip gleamed bright red. Suddenly, they were surrounded by an eye-searing cone of light as a searchbeam locked onto them. Raffi was too surprised to act, but Milla pulled him to her with surprising strength, so they rolled down the slope a second before a snake of red fire arced down through the beam and made a crater of the area where they had just lain.

Rubble fell and bounced all around them. Trying to

remain conscious and moving, Raffi dragged himself to his feet, then pulled her up, too. He hauled her towards the shell of the building where he'd seen Sal disappear a moment before. Milla had no movement in her legs. The toes of her blood-spattered feet dragged behind her. He hauled her through a window and they collapsed in the remains of the Info Centre. Hologrammatic images of silently talking heads alongside mathematical symbols and chunks of text revolved surreally through the dust-laden air above them as they lay on the cracked and broken floor. Through the twinkling, turning kaleidoscope, Raffi could see dark sky between the broken beams of the ceiling. He took off his helmet. It felt strangely peaceful lying there gazing up at this sight, with the injured warrior girl next to him. Outside, the thud and screech of battle seemed far away.

'Thankyou,' he murmured to her.

'We did good, din't we, racer-boy?' Her words sounded choked, her breathing strained.

'You okay?'

She chuckled. 'We looked out for each other, din't we?'

There was something very wrong with her voice, as though life was leaking out of her with every word. With effort he turned to look at her, and through the gap in her jacket, saw the deep shiny-red hollow in her abdomen. The wound looked serious. 'Your lance,' she managed to say. 'Fell on it when I crashed.'

'We'll get you to the Med Centre,' Raffi said.

Milla struggled to smile. 'Hold me,' she asked. He turned and embraced her, pulling her to him, feeling the warm, slow surge of her blood against his body.

Minutes went by. The sounds of the battle slowly faded. Sal arrived. She crouched down next to Raffi and tried to pull him from Milla's body. He didn't want to let go – not yet.

'She's dead,' Sal said coldly.

Raffi sniffed, finally sitting up. The front of his jacket dripped with blood. He gently removed Milla's helmet, smoothing down her black and red hair.

'Where are Dario and Jonah?' Sal asked.

'I don't know.'

'We'd better get going,' she said. 'We're in enemy territory, and they could come for us at any time. Which way to Pennyminder's store?'

Sal's relentlessness finally got to Raffi. 'We have to look for Jonah and Dario,' he told her. 'Or don't you care about them any more?'

She looked at him, eyes suddenly ablaze with emotion he didn't dare interpret. Then she said very quietly: 'We have to keep moving. It's our only chance.'

She took the gun from Milla's thigh holster and stuffed it into her belt. 'Come on,' she ordered.

CHAPTER SIXTEEN

⌛

FLEETING AVENUE

utside, on Fleeting Avenue, the battle was over. Raffi counted the wrecks of five maroon bikes and half a dozen black ones. There may have been others, it was hard to be sure with so much rubble, dust and smoke. The Suicide Squad had turned out to be just that – perhaps not one of them had survived. Sal didn't seem remotely concerned about the human cost of her brilliant plan – it had brought her a step closer to her goal, and that was all she cared about.

'Where now?' asked Sal.

Raffi felt numb, as if another kind of desyncronisation device had shifted him a few degrees north of his own feelings. Perhaps he'd been infected by Sal's insensitivity, or perhaps he was simply too overwhelmed by everything, and an essential part of himself had shut down. He probably looked the same, and was able to think logically enough about how to get to Pennyminder's store. He could still move nimbly, as he picked his way over the rubble, leading Sal in what he hoped was the right direction. But within him, just a few unfired neurons away, he sensed this vast wall of stuff – shock, fear, anger, sadness – waiting to sweep him over.

Fleeting Avenue was one long bombsite with more craters than intact buildings. It marked the battered frontline of an ongoing territorial battle between Potter Logan and Austra Bella. Right now, though, Logan's troops were far to the south-east, engaged in a fight for control of their heartland. Way off to his left, Raffi could see the deadly crimson threads and hear the muffled thumps and cries of battle over Hawking Hills and Transient Ridge: more pointless deaths in a petty tribal squabble over a doomed world. And Austra Bella, where was she? This was her chance surely. Raffi looked to his right, almost willing the gangster queen to show herself. But he saw nothing in the shadows beyond the ruins.

It was hard to recognise landmarks in such a changed setting, but just enough familiar frontages had survived for Raffi to navigate by. Eventually, they came to a place where the avenue broadened. Benches arranged around empty, blasted flowerbeds and saplings – now withered and leafless – told him they had arrived.

To the right, taking up some five metres of frontage, should have been Parsim Pennyminder's store. It wasn't there. Raffi took a step closer, kicked absently at a foothill of the mountain of rubble that had taken the retail unit's place. He turned to Sal. 'Somewhere under here,' he told her, 'is the access shaft.'

Sal went down slowly on her haunches so that the large gun rose up on her stomach. She picked up a stone and threw it at the great mound. From the look on her face, Raffi guessed she might be about to scream, but she held her breath. The mound was enormous. It would take weeks to shift it with their bare hands – weeks they didn't have. And the shaft may not even have survived beneath it.

'No other way down, right?'

'Not that I know of.'

She picked up a brick from the mound and threw it over her shoulder; then another one. Her frail shoulders tensed as she lifted a larger concrete block and heaved it with all her strength to a place two or three metres away. She was clearly insane, maybe even more so than him. In a different state of mind he might have felt foolish watching this undersized girl sweating away, with him not lifting a finger. But such feelings had no power over him now. He could have watched her quite happily for hours, and might have done had a man with a gun not suddenly shouted 'Halt!'

The green-helmeted figure, wearing a pair of utterly redundant sunglasses, had appeared at the top of the rubble mound. He had them both in the sights of his flamegun. 'Identify yourselves. This is Bella's Domain.'

'They're just a bunch of looters,' came a higher, more nasal voice. Raffi turned to his left to see another green helmet atop a round, red face. 'You know the rules. Let's kill 'em.'

A low drone, which had been gathering at the edges of Raffi's consciousness for some minutes, was getting gradually more insistent.

'They might know something,' argued Sunglasses. 'Maybe we should question them first. Then we can kill them.'

'You guys know anything?' asked Red Face.

'What do you want to know?' said Sal.

The drone continued to rise in volume.

'Just start talking and we'll tell you if we're interested.' Red Face looked bored with the conversation, and itching to pull his trigger.

'Potter Logan's fighting Red Oakes for control of Transient Ridge and Hawking Hills,' said Sal. 'His northern guard has already been badly weakened in a battle on Fleeting just south of here. You can tell your leader that Periodic Park is ripe for the taking.'

The green helmets looked at each other and laughed. 'And that's supposed to be news, is it?' giggled Red Face. The drone was now almost deafening. He pointed his flamegun upwards, and Raffi looked aloft to see a sky full of dark green, armoured bikes trailing their purple plasma clouds. There had to be well over a hundred, progressing in broad ranks south-east, towards Periodic Park: a full-scale invasion force that spelt doom for Logan, not to mention Red's expansion plans.

'So,' said Sunglasses. 'You were about to tell us something we don't know. Well go on then, we're all ears.'

Sal looked lost for a moment. Then she glanced at the mound she was standing on and one eyebrow went up. 'Actually we do have some information you might find interesting: this pile used to be a cosmetic store. Underneath it is a cellar full of equipment that could be useful for treating the battle-scarred among you. If you help us remove all this rubble—'

Red Face scoffed. 'We wear our battle scars with pride around here. Now if you two don't come up with something really useful in the next few seconds, we'll seriously have to kill you.'

'There's an access shaft,' sighed Raffi. He ignored the black looks coming from Sal, not particularly caring any more what she thought of him. 'Below the cellar is a vertical shaft that leads down to a massive underground prison network, with enormous kitchens full of food. If you can get down there you'll have enough food and drink to last you and your tribe for years.'

Red Face looked sceptical. 'What bull is this?'

'It may not be bull,' said Sunglasses. 'I remember Pennyminder saying something about a shaft before we did him.'

'Well they've told us about it now, Ash, so we don't need 'em.' Red Face aimed his gun at Sal.

Red Face didn't look as though he was joking, and Ash didn't look bothered enough to intervene. The urgency of the situation finally penetrated Raffi's benumbed heart. 'Wait,' he said. 'This shaft is very well hidden. You'll need our help to locate it.'

'Total bull,' smiled Red Face, and his finger closed around the trigger.

'Cool it, McBride,' shouted Ash. 'We can't take the chance. The kid might be telling the truth. Now we're going to need an earthmover to shift this stuff. Let's take these kids back to base and we can plan what to do from there.'

McBride reluctantly moved forward and removed the weapon from Sal's belt, while keeping the gun trained on her. Then he prodded her in the back with the muzzle. 'Get moving, the both of you.'

CHAPTER SEVENTEEN

⧖

AT THE COURT OF QUEEN BELLA

They walked and stumbled across the ruins of the old market district that lay between Fleeting and Season. The charred and broken remains of stalls lay strewn across the cobblestones, their wares long since looted. They arrived, at last, at the holoplex on Season Square, which looked remarkably intact compared to the smashed-up buildings around it. 'In here,' ordered McBride, and he and Ash pushed their captives through the building's entrance. The doors still swished open and shut as though nothing had changed since the days when Raffi, Dario and Sal came here for an evening's entertainment.

A uniformed guard approached them, one of at least a dozen guarding a second set of doors, leading to 'Auditorium One', the holoplex's main viewing chamber. 'Who are they?' asked the dark-skinned guard. He was young, perhaps Raffi's age, but seemed remarkably assured. His olive green uniform was crisp and new and his face was smooth but for a neat and well-trimmed beard – in vivid contrast to Red's followers with their dirty facial hair and tatty, improvised uniforms. How, Raffi wondered, did a sophisticated tribe like Austra Bella's suddenly arise in the eleven days that had elapsed since the Malfunction? Where did the uniforms come from? The weapons? The organization? Who had this guard been eleven days ago? An ordinary young joe, like Raffi? Surely not. It was almost as though the whole thing had been planned a long way in advance.

'Picked them up on Fleeting,' reported Ash. 'They claim there's a shaft under Pennyminder's store leading to a stash of food.'

'To which tribe do they belong?'

Ash looked embarrassed. 'We didn't ask them. We assumed they were a couple of tribeless looters.'

The guard turned to Raffi. 'What is your tribe?'

Raffi hesitated, unsure of the best response, and Sal quickly answered for him. 'We belong to no tribe,' she said, 'and we wish you no ill. We simply want to go our own way in peace.'

McBride chuckled. 'For tribeless, they certainly knew a lot about the fight between Logan and Oakes for control of the west.'

The guard looked suspicious. 'Tell us about this food store under Fleeting.'

'Well,' said Raffi, 'there's this prison system on the Underside, and–'

'Wait!' The guard held up his hand. He looked alarmed. Glancing swiftly at Ash and McBride, he said to them, 'Okay, you two get back out on patrol.'

'What about the shaft?' asked Ash. 'Do you want us to–?'

'Never mind about that. Just get back on Fleeting. There may be some refugees after the recent engagement that will need dealing with.'

When Ash and McBride were gone, the guard leaned close to Raffi and Sal. 'You two know more than you ought to about the Underside,' he said. Then he turned to a colleague, equally well turned out, and beckoned him over. 'Watch these two a minute, will you?' The first guard wandered off, speaking discreetly into his wearable. He kept glancing back at Raffi and Sal, and Raffi thought he overheard him describing their appearance. A minute later, he returned. 'You,' he announced, 'have the honour of an audience with Queen Bella. Follow me, please.'

The guards stood aside and the doors to Auditorium One hissed open. The auditorium was familiar to Raffi from the many visits he'd made there to watch comedy or drama holoflicks. But usually the lights were off to allow for better viewing of the movie. The circular tiers of seating surrounding the central space would normally be full of customers enjoying the spectacle. Today, though, the seats were empty and the lights were on, and in the centre, in place of hologrammatic movie entertainment, was a high platform surrounded by four armed guards wearing the same well-cut green uniforms as those outside. On top of the platform, seated on a large, ceremonial chair, was Queen Austra Bella. Or, as Raffi and Sal knew her, Lastara Blue.

When he saw her, Raffi involuntarily rushed forwards. 'Lastara! How?' One of the guards immediately grabbed him and pushed him back towards the edge of the chamber. Lastara only smiled dreamily. She lounged comfortably against the back of her enormous throne in her robe of metallic pink with a blue collar, and boots to match. Perched at an angle on her head was a small gold filigree crown topped with star shapes filled with multi-coloured precious stones. 'Hello, my sweethearts,' she breathed. 'I thought it was you out there. The description fitted. And no one else would have known about the Underside.'

'Stupid of me,' said Sal. 'I should have realised that Austra Bella is an anagram of Lastara Blue!'

Raffi, aware he was gaping like a fish, couldn't help the stream of questions gushing out of him. 'What happened to you Lastara? How did you get to be Austra Bella? How did you become a gangster queen? We only lost you three days ago. You simply couldn't have risen so far so fast.'

'Oh Raffi,' she laughed. 'You know so little, don't you. You assumed for all those days and weeks I was just idling away my life, shopping and modelling and getting high… Well, actually, you're right. That's what I did spend most of my time doing. But you know me, darling, I've always been a people person, I like people – okay, I like men! And they usually like me.' She smiled coyly at him. 'I have a contact, a very powerful contact, at Secrocon HQ. It was he who rescued me from Red's thugs and very kindly brought me here. And it was he who helped me to become queen of this tribe. And what a wonderful-looking queen I make, don't you think?' She stood up and treated them to a slow twirl, making her robe flare outwards at the bottom and the jewels in her crown twinkle in the overhead lights. 'You know, my father always told me I could be anyone I wanted. I bet he never imagined I'd end up a queen!'

As he watched her foolishness, Raffi wondered how a girl like Lastara could have so effortlessly risen to this position – effectively the most powerful person on the Topside. He could see that Sal was thinking the same thing. 'What happened to the previous ruler of this tribe?' She struggled to recall the name Lars had mentioned. 'Stimson someone?'

'Oh, Stimson Grebe wasn't very understanding unfortunately,' said Lastara. 'He couldn't be made to see that only I as leader could provide the soldiers, weapons and equipment to make us the most powerful tribe in the Chronosphere. He had to be dispatched to the Underside for a spot of re-education.'

Just then the guard who had brought them in earlier reappeared. 'Queen Bella,' he bowed.

'Yes, what is it, Faroukh?'

'I bring good news, your Highness. Our forces have wiped out Logan and taken possession of the north-west. We are still encountering some scattered resistance from Oakes, but the field commanders describe it as a "mopping-up exercise". We hope to be in full possession of Solstice Park within the next 24 hours.'

'Thankyou, Faroukh, you sweet man. Let me know if you need any more men or guns or anything, won't you?'

'Of course, your Highness. I should also inform you that we have picked up another refugee on Fleeting. He claims to have been one of four, two of whom fit the description of your current guests. Shall I show him in?"

Raffi's heart leapt. It had to be Dario or Jonah.

'Yes, please do.'

Dario entered. He had dirt and blood on his face, but otherwise looked intact. On seeing Lastara, he did a double-take just like Raffi and Sal had done earlier. 'Lastara! What do you know? I always suspected you had a touch of the blue in your veins!' He turned to Sal and Raffi. 'Hey!' he cried, opening his arms to them and grinning broadly.

Raffi embraced him. Then Sal, more hesitantly, reached up and touched Dario's blood-stained cheek, almost as if to test it was really him.

'I can't believe you survived – again!' cried Raffi.

'Nine lives, mate! What can I say! My rider, Baz, was hit in the scuffle over Transient, and we limped along with you guys as far as Spell Street, then got blasted by some balcony snipers as we ran in towards Lower Fleeting. Baz didn't make it, sadly.'

'Faroukh,' said Lastara. 'Could you organise some jasmine tea sorbets and sugary snacks for my friends here. And some bowls of water so they can clean themselves up.'

Faroukh bowed and left.

'Any sign of Jonah?' enquired Dario.

'Nothing, I'm afraid.'

'Jonah was also with you?' For the first time, a hint of concern furrowed Lastara's brow.

'We may have to accept that he's dead,' said Raffi bleakly. 'We had two battles with Logan's forces and I don't think one of our squadron escort survived. It's actually a miracle that three of us made it through.'

Lastara was quiet for a moment as she absorbed this. Her eyes seemed to be far away. Then she recalled herself. 'Perhaps,' she said, 'you'd like to explain why in hooly you decided to embark on such an absurdly dangerous flight. Was Red's hospitality not up to scratch?'

Sal explained about her search for her sister and Raffi's belief that she may be imprisoned in the Re-Education Centre. 'We were trying to get to the Underside,' she concluded.

'Oh, Sal, I wish you'd told me about this months ago. I might have been able to help you then, but I think it very unlikely she's still there now. Once re-education is complete, all inmates enter the Seed Race, from whose bourne, I'm afraid, no traveller returns.'

'Okay you've lost me there,' said Sal.

Lastara sighed, putting her fingers together in front of her, teacher-style. 'The Seed Race,' she explained, 'is the real purpose of the Chronosphere. They're the chosen ones whose task is to build a new and better world here, safely insulated from the corrupt and violent one outside. The Topside pleasure dome was only created as a bait to draw the right sort of people in. The target market for the resort was teenagers, especially the rebellious and carefree types who fancied a bit of time away from their parents and schoolwork and Vocational Training. As you know, the Chronosphere was very successful at attracting them... Ah, thank-you

Faroukh.' She broke off as he and some other guards entered with the tea things and bowls of water. 'Faroukh is on secondment from Secrocon, aren't you Faroukh? He's one of hundreds provided to me by my Secrocon contact, Chrono-Sensei Avon Drak.' At the mention of this name, Raffi exchanged a quick glance with Sal.

One of the throne room guards mounted the steps to hand Lastara her dish. 'Thankyou gorgeous,' Lastara winked at him. She took a mouthful of her sorbet before continuing. 'My job, and those of my colleagues, was to find the best and brightest young boys and girls and dispatch them for re-education. Once they've been fully indoctrinated, they receive an audience with our leader the Chronomaster and join the Seed Race. They're sent to live in the Garden...' Her eyes softened as she mentioned the last word. 'The Garden is a beautiful place – a kind of paradise on earth. I hope one day you three will get to see it. Then you'll understand why all that you've had to go through these past few weeks was worth it. In the Garden, the Seed Race will eventually breed and produce a new generation of Chronospheric children who will never have known life outside of the paradise – the Celestial Sphere – we're creating. Their lives will be perfect.'

'Where is this Garden?' asked Sal, as she wiped the dirt from her face with a damp cloth.

'It's at the base of the Sphere. But it's enormous and full of light and air and music and the most delicious food you'll ever eat. A hundred paradisiacs couldn't make you as happy as an hour spent in the Garden.'

Raffi was unimpressed. 'And the heat,' he said, 'the disease, the gangs and the slaughter going on around us – I suppose that's all part of the plan too, is it?'

'It wasn't quite planned that way,' replied Lastara, her dreamy expression momentarily clouded with regret. 'Once Secrocon had filled their Seed Race quota and no longer required new blood, they closed the temp-al chambers to fully isolate the Chronosphere from the outside world. It was called the Malfunction, but it was quite deliberate. The chaos that followed was an unfortunate side-effect of that event.'

Lastara's smile returned as she added: 'But Secrocon solved the problem by installing me, their most loyal follower, as queen of the most powerful Topside tribe. As you heard from Faroukh, we've nearly completed the task of bringing the dissident tribes to heel, and we can soon go forward to the next phase of the project: the orderly abandonment of the Topside. Eventually, the Topside will be rebuilt as an Upper Garden, giving more space to the burgeoning population of the Seed Race. And that, my dear friends, is the truth of the Chronosphere, and the reason why I, of all people, find myself looking down upon you now as queen!'

Raffi cut himself a slice of his green apple foam frittercake. He thought about what he'd just heard. Lastara's story sounded plausible, and certainly explained a few things – the teen kidnappings, the Re-Ed Centre, the Malfunction, as well as her sudden reappearance as leader of a large and well-organised tribe. But whatever the truth of her words, and however wonderful this Garden was, it couldn't possibly excuse the catastrophic suffering and loss of life of the past eleven days.

Faroukh re-entered. 'Your highness,' he bowed. 'The Chrono-Sensei requests an audience.'

'Of course. Please send him in.'

Almost before she had finished speaking, Avon Drak brushed past Faroukh and swept into the auditorium. The last time Raffi had seen him was seven months before in the Desynchronisation Suite of the Re-Ed Centre, and he was struck again by the man's strange yet impressive physical appearance: tall, with an upright bearing and a strong-boned and handsome brown face, he instantly commanded people's attention. But what really drew the eye was his white-blond hair, and the vividly contrasting streak of darkness that swept down through the left side of his head, ending with a black spot in his eyebrow like the dot on an exclamation mark.

Avon surveyed the room, his cold, grey eyes assessing Dario, Sal and Raffi in turn. He looked like someone suppressing a great deal of anger. 'My dear,' he said eventually, turning to Lastara. 'I realise these are old friends of yours, but you have no business associating with them now – not in your current position. Two of them are fugitives from justice, and the other one…' He looked at Sal. 'I've had my suspicions about her for quite some time.'

'Avon, sweetie, I think it's my business who I associate with. I'm queen, after all.'

He swivelled towards her so Raffi could no longer see his expression, only the menacing tautness of his shoulder muscles. 'Just remember who made you queen, sweetie,' he said softly. 'Now I want you to send the three of them to the Punishment and Experimentation Centre. I shall expect to see them there within the hour.'

Lastara's face fell. 'Punishment and Exp… You mean the Re-Education Centre, surely?'

'No. The Re-Ed Centre is for people who are ready for re-education. For persistent miscreants we have other facilities, which are much less pleasant.' Glancing back at the miscreants, he added: 'A spell in the PEC should sort this lot out – it never fails. I'm sure when you see them again, they'll be changed for the better, and thoroughly keen on the idea of re-education.'

Lastara sat back on her throne, looking shocked, almost scared. 'Avon, I don't understand. You never told me about any of this before.'

Avon's stance softened. Slowly, with head bowed, he mounted the platform steps to where Lastara sat. He took her hand, then gently touched her cheek. She looked up at him, her pale, liquid-blue eyes – usually so dreamily confident about everything – now fearful and childlike. 'There are some things, my dear, I've had to shield you from,' he murmered. 'Some necessary activities that aren't so easily understood by a mind as beautiful and delicate as yours. To create a perfect world – the world we've often talked about – we must first remove all imperfections, even if we find ourselves growing attached to some of those... imperfections. Most young people are easily perfectable. For some it takes a little longer. You must say goodbye to your friends, Lastara. It'll be a while before they're ready to join us on our journey to the Celestial Sphere.'

CHAPTER EIGHTEEN

ROYAL ESCORT

hen Drak had gone, Lastara sat on her throne for a long time with her elbows on the armrests and her face shielded by her hands, as if not daring to look her friends in the eye. Finally, when she looked up, there were tears on her cheeks. She plucked the crown from her head and gazed at it for a while, before flicking it away from her. The flimsy ornament bounced once on the platform edge before rattling to the floor.

'As you can see,' she sniffed to her audience, 'I'm not really queen at all. I don't have any real power. Avon only gave me the job because I have a superficial charm, a way with people, and… as a favour to a friend. We go back a long way, Avon and I. Even further back than me and Jonah, actually.' She sniffed again and rubbed her cheek. 'Poor Jonah… But that's another story. Dario, Sal, Raffi, I'm so sorry. It seems I can send out armies and wreak havoc on the Topside, but I have no power over what becomes of you, my dearest, sweetest friends. I must do as Avon bids. I just hope this Punishment and Experimentation Centre isn't as frightful as it sounds. Please, please promise me, all of you, not to be brave. Just do whatever they tell you and say whatever they want you to say, and I'm sure you'll be out of there in a matter of days. Then we'll all be able to join the Seed Race together.'

Lastara rose to her feet and descended the platform to the floor. She went to Dario first, taking his hands in hers and kissing him on his now-cleaner cheek. Then she crossed the floor to Raffi. 'Take care of the others for me,' she whispered in his ear. 'I'll see you soon.' She kissed him.

As she moved away, Raffi caught a flash of something moving in Sal's hand. Lastara, not seeing this, smiled encouragingly at her. When she embraced her, she kept a slight distance, sensitive to Sal's dislike of close physical contact. Into this gap between their bodies, Raffi saw the flash of cool yellow metal reappear. He recognized it as a small knife – they had each been given one with their sweet snacks. The sharp end was now pressing firmly into Lastara's abdomen.

Lastara's eyes flipped open in alarm. But before she could say anything, Sal had spun her around and pinned her arm behind her, now placing the knife blade against her throat. Lastara was a lot taller than her assailant, so she was forced into an awkward posture, arched backwards against Sal's right shoulder. The four guards on sentry duty around the platform immediately moved towards Sal, their guns raised.

'Stand back!' screamed Sal, pushing the knife blade harder into the flesh of Lastara's neck and making her stagger and cry out in pain. 'Move another centimetre and I'll kill your queen.' The men froze. 'Right,' said Sal. 'That's better! Now throw your weapons on the floor.' The guards hesitated, exchanging quick, nervous glances with one another. 'Do it!' yelled Sal, and she made a slice with the blade so that a thin line of blood appeared on Lastara's neck. 'Just do what she says,' their queen croaked. Four guns clattered to the floor. Raffi and Dario quickly picked up two each. Dario pocketed one while keeping the other aimed at the guards. Raffi handed one of his to Sal, who then pushed Lastara away from her and aimed the gun at her instead.

'Sal, darling, please!' begged Lastara, nursing the red mark on her neck. 'This is pointless. You'll be captured immediately. This place will be teeming with soldiers–'

'Silence!' cried Sal, smacking her hard across the face. 'From now on, you'll speak when you're spoken to. Understand?'

Lastara nodded meekly. She looked stunned.

Sal now turned to the guards. 'Take off your uniforms,' she ordered. She knows exactly what she's doing, thought Raffi, impressed. She must have worked it all out in her head beforehand. The guards hastily undressed, and Raffi saw that they were just callow youths like him – like everyone he had so far encountered in Drak's teen empire. Raffi, seeing Sal's plan, began stripping off his own clothes so he could change into one of the guards' uniforms.

Dario quickly followed suit. 'What about you, Sal?' he asked.

'I'm not going to fool anyone in a uniform,' she replied. 'Not with this hair. You two will be the royal escort; I'll be Queen Bella's friend who she's taking on a tour of the Underside.'

Dario's jacket was too tight and Raffi's trousers were too short – Raffi wasn't confident their turn as the new royal escort would fool anyone. Then he had an inspiration. 'We could use our CID masks, hey Dario? That way they'll see who they expect to see wearing these uniforms.'

'Great idea, mate.' They switched on the pulse beam regulators on the backs of their belts.

'Is there a stun mode on these guns?' Sal asked the guards, now standing around awkwardly in their underwear.

None of them answered.

'If you don't tell me,' she said impatiently, 'I shall just have to kill you.'

Eventually one stepped forwards. 'They're temp fi-ers,' he explained stutteringly. 'They work by erasing or distorting people's temporal fields. There's no stun mode but you can send us into... into a temporary time-loop if you like.' He pointed to a particular setting on the dial at the back of the weapon. 'It just means we experience the same period of time again and again.'

Sal rotated the dial. 'What are these flashing numbers?' she asked, pointing at a small screen above the dial.

'That allows you to set the number of minutes you want each time-loop to last.'

'I'll make it five seconds,' she said, setting the stop-clock. 'I don't want to give you any chance of raising the alarm. Oh Jeebus, now what's this number?'

'That's the total number of minutes you want to keep us looping for.'

'Half an hour should do it,' muttered Sal as she keyed in the number. Then she told them to go and stand in a group in the far corner of the auditorium. The men sloped off and waited dejectedly as she took aim and fired. A pink cone of light briefly enclosed them, then disappeared. The men continued to stand there, seemingly unaffected.

'Start walking towards me, boys,' ordered Sal.

They began to walk, but no sooner had they started than they were back where they'd begun. The switch was instant, like a piece of motion media trickery. They set out again, and after taking just three or four paces towards the centre of the room, they abruptly vanished and reappeared back in the corner.

'Okay, it's working. Now, let's get out of here. Lastara, are you ready? You're queen, remember?' She picked up Lastara's fallen crown and handed it to her. 'If anyone asks where you're going, tell them you're taking me to the Garden.'

'Why the Garden?'

'Because that's where I think my sister is, and that's where we're going.'

'I can't take you to the Garden, Sal sweetie. It wouldn't be allowed. Only the Seed Race can enter the Garden, and neither of us qualify.'

Sal snorted. 'For a queen, your powers don't extend very far!'

'I thought we'd established that,' said Lastara, looking down.

'Well how close to it can you get us?'

'I can take you to Secrocon HQ. That's as deep into the Sphere as I've ever been. In fact it's at the very centre.'

'Is that close to the Garden?'

'A lot closer than we are now.'

'Well then let's go. Come on.'

They headed towards the auditorium exit – Lastara and Sal next to each other in the centre, Raffi to their left, Dario to their right. Behind them, the four guards continued their abortive attempts to get more than four paces from the far corner.

⧗

Queen Bella, together with her guest and royal escort, swished through the doors and strode at a swift pace across the foyer. The faces of the guards, as they passed, were impassive. None noticed the escorts' ill-fitting uniforms nor the gun Bella's guest was discreetly pointing at her back.

CHRONOSPHERE

On the far side of the holoplex foyer was a pair of doors that in former days Raffi recalled had always been locked. Today the doors slid open at a touch of Lastara's thumb to the scanpad. They revealed a functional concrete room housing a levitator dome – a round-topped transparent column protruding some three metres above floor level. A pellucid door within the column hissed upwards and they stepped inside, onto the hovering light disc that dipped slightly under the weight of each new entrant. 'Secrocon HQ,' instructed Lastara, and – her voiceprint having checked out – the light disc began its swift descent towards the Underside.

CHAPTER NINETEEN

SECROCON HQ

The light disc plummeted at high speed through a black, featureless shaft.

'Sweetie, you can quit digging a hole in my back with that thing,' Lastara complained. 'I'm hardly going to take on the three of you, am I?'

'Shut up,' said Sal. 'Unless you fancy getting your temporal field splattered all over this levitator.'

'I just can't believe we were ever friends, darling. What's got into you? Was it something I said?'

'Quit trying to psyche me and just think about what you're going to say to the Secrocon guys when we get there.'

'Oh, don't worry about that,' smiled Lastara, who seemed to have regained some of her customary insouciance. 'I'm a people person, remember? I can handle anyone.'

Every ten seconds or so on their long downward journey they caught brief glimpses of rooms and corridors, but they were falling too fast to get a proper look at them.

'I had no idea this place was so big,' murmured Raffi. 'We must have gone deeper by now than the total height of the Topside.'

'Oh, the Topside is only a very small part of the Sphere,' said Lastara. 'The tip of the iceberg one might say. Avon once told me you could easily fit 18 Topsides into the entire thing. The diameter of the whole Sphere is around ten kilometres, or ten Time Towers piled on top of one another.'

Raffi was reminded of Septimus Watts and his ambitions to chart the entire Underside. The poor guy had merely scratched the surface. The place was bigger than any of them could have imagined. The engineering involved in creating it simply boggled the mind.

Finally, the levitator began to slow and they emerged from the gloomy shaft into a bright space – almost too bright to look at, and they were forced, at first, to squint. The breath caught in Raffi's throat as his eyes gradually adjusted to the view that now confronted them. He'd never seen anything so magnificent in all his life. They were descending through a transparent tube into an enormous, hollow, white spherical space, perhaps a kilometre in diameter. All around them were transparent spheres, like enormous bubbles – at least twenty of them – with levitator shafts interconnecting them and holding them in place to form a giant three-dimensional lattice. At the very centre of the space was a larger sphere with a surface of shiny, reflective chrome. Like the others, this was linked to its neighbours by levitator shafts. Inside each of the 'bubbles' (as Raffi immediately thought of them) and moving along on light discs inside the levitator shafts, he could see hundreds of tiny grey-uniformed figures. Each bubble had an upper and lower floor filled with control panels, machinery and hologrammatic images, which were being manipulated or monitored by the uniformed workers. It added up to an extraordinary vision of teeming, hive-like industry within a setting of stark, geometric beauty.

'Secrocon HQ!' breathed Lastara. 'Stunning, isn't it?'

'Truly!' said Dario, who was the first of the others to rediscover his voice.

'Everything in the Sphere is controlled from here,' explained Lastara, 'from the speed of time to the menus in the Lower Atrium eathouses.'

Their light disc slid slowly into the nearest transparent sphere, coming to rest in the centre of its upper floor. The levitator door slid upwards.

'Careful now,' Sal whispered to Lastara as they filed out. She kept the gun firmly pressed to her back.

The room was dominated by a tall, slowly rotating hourglass, like a miniature Time Tower. Its matt black surface was covered in intricate recessed symbols that illuminated and faded every few seconds. This was accompanied by a dull throbbing sound that rose and fell in volume in sync with the lights.

One of the grey uniforms approached them. He had an O-shaped mouth and a smooth, pink, hairless head. From the gold braiding on his jacket, he looked senior. 'Queen Bella, what a pleasant surprise,' said the man, giving a small bow.

'Chief Pundit Pilo Metis,' curtsied Lastara. 'A pleasure as always.' Her smile made him glow yet more pinkly. 'May I introduce my dear friend Sal Morrow. I'm just giving her a quick tour of Sec HQ. I hope that's alright?'

Metis looked unsure. 'Does she have sufficient security clearance?'

'As if you needed to ask, Pilo,' laughed Lastara. 'Of course she has.'

He relaxed and his mouth become slightly less circular. 'Well that should be fine then. If your friend wouldn't mind just placing her thumb on the scanpad here, and if everything checks out, we can let you go on your way.'

Raffi held his breath, watching Sal to see what she would do next. Her thumbprint wouldn't check out and would most likely raise an alarm: they should all have been in the Punishment and Experimentation Centre by now. Sal glanced at him and then, after a brief flick around the room, her eyes dropped to the gun in his belt. He could see what she was planning. Besides Pilo, there were just three others in the upper part of the bubble: one human and two that looked like D-grade androids – manual workers with limited intelligence and, hopefully, slow reflexes.

Sal stepped from behind Lastara, as if heading towards the scanpad. But as she did so, she revealed to Pilo the gun in her hand. The man gasped.

'Stay quiet,' she hissed. 'Don't move, and show no alarm.'

Raffi and Dario reached for their own guns and levelled them at the others in the room. The human technician ceased his work and simply stood in startled silence. The androids didn't react at all. This was not an eventuality they had been programmed to deal with, so they ignored it.

'What do you want with us?' asked Pilo Metis.

'Your cooperation,' answered Sal. 'I want you to get us into the Garden.'

'I can't do that. Only Seed Race can enter the Garden.'

'That's what I told her,' said Lastara.

'Shut up!' Sal rasped at her. She turned back to Pilo. 'If you don't come up with a way of getting us into the Garden very quickly, I shall start shooting this gun at everyone and everything in this room.'

Pilo looked distraught – the skin of his face was soft, pink and sweat-glazed around the doughnut hole of his mouth. 'I- I honestly can't help.'

A bleeper went off on his collar, making him jump.

'Answer it,' whispered Sal.

Pilo, frightened eyes still staring at her, lowered his head. 'Yes?'

'Sphere 14 here, Chief Pundit,' came the compressed voice

from the tiny speaker. 'TV has slipped to 3.8 in Sector 4. Can you adjust?'

Sal nodded at him.

'Yes, no problem,' he replied. A bleep indicated the caller had disconnected. 'I have to make an adjustment to temporal velocity,' Pilo told Sal. 'If I don't do it right now, it will attract attention.'

'Do it. But no funny business, or I start shooting, okay?'

Pilo pressed some keys on his workstation, sending a brief shimmer of colour through the black hourglass in the centre of the room. Then he dived for cover under the workstation. At the same moment, the light everywhere darkened to a pulsating, blood-red glow as a deafening siren went off. Outside the bubble, Raffi saw that the whole of Sec HQ had become suffused with the same deep-red light, which emanated from each bubble and even from the levitator tubes. Wherever he looked, grey-uniformed figures were rushing from one place to another, no doubt following prearranged emergency protocols. A robotic female voice boomed out across the cavernous space: 'Lockdown! Lockdown!' it echoed. 'Suspected enemy infiltration of Sphere 12. All available fighter units advance to Sphere 12 for immediate intercept of infiltrators. Border Control: institute immediate blockade on all traffic to and from Sec HQ.'

A flash of white-hot energy burst outwards from the muzzle of Sal's gun, thudding into the human technician and sending him flying. He hung in the air like a sculpted representation of pure shock and fear, flickering in and out of existence for a three or four seconds, before fading away entirely.

Raffi couldn't conceal his shock as he stared disbelievingly at the empty space that had once contained a living, breathing man. 'You've – you've just killed him!'

'Not just killed him,' murmured Dario. 'Erased him in time, as though he never existed.'

Sal crouched down beneath the workstation where Pilo was cowering and pointed the gun at his sweating forehead. 'Tell them it was an error – or else the next one'll be for you.'

'I–I can't. Once emergency procedures have been set in motion, they're impossible to stop.'

The whine of light discs could be heard approaching from at least three different directions.

'Think about it, Chief Pundit,' warned Sal. 'When I pull this trigger, which I will in the next five seconds, your mother will never have known you. Your children will never have been born.'

Light discs manned by heavily armed and armoured droids shot into the room from above and on all sides of them. Raffi saw Sal's finger slowly squeezing the trigger. She didn't look like she was bluffing.

'Okay, okay,' cried Pilo. 'I'll tell them it was a mistake.'

Sal's gun-holding hand moved inside her jacket but the gun remained pointing at Pilo as the first droids began emerging from the shaft. Pilo jumped to his feet and rushed to the lead droid. 'I'm sorry,' he said. 'It was a mistake. There's no emergency.'

'Our orders are to detain everyone in this sphere.'

'Well let me countermand those orders.' He ran back to his workstation and began pressing buttons while talking frantically into his collar stud: 'This is Chief Pundit Pilo Metis,' he shouted. 'Security passcode 54610. I made an error. I'm very sorry. This is a false alarm.'

There was a long pause, then the siren died and the light in Sec HQ returned to normal. The fighter droids returned to the levitators and departed. 'Your incompetence has caused severe disruption,' came a voice from Pilo's wearable. The voice sounded high, rich and melodious, even compressed as it was by the tiny speaker in his collar. 'I'm not happy with you, Chief Pundit. A warning will go on your file.'

Pilo sighed. 'I understand, Chronomaster.'

CHAPTER TWENTY

THE CHRONOMASTER

nder Sal's close supervision, Pilo deactivated the two droids and wiped their memories of all the events of the previous fifteen minutes. 'Now, Chief Pundit,' said Sal. 'Take us to the Garden.'

The man looked ten years closer to the grave as she prodded him towards the nearest levitator shaft. Raffi was now on Lastara-watch, keeping his eyes and gun carefully trained on her as they followed Sal, Pilo and Dario onto the light disc. He was still reeling from the memory of Sal's cold-blooded action, and the new levels of ruthlessness that it had revealed in this slight and ordinary-seeming girl.

The light disc plunged towards the big chrome ball – Raffi estimated its diameter at around 100 metres – at the centre of Secrocon HQ. 'The only way of getting into the Garden is from there,' Pilo explained, gesturing towards the rapidly approaching sphere. 'Sec HQ Central – the office of the Chronomaster. He controls all access to the Garden. You can't get in there without going through him. All I can do is take you there.'

'You'd better do more than that, Chief Pundit,' growled Sal. 'Start thinking of a story, and quickly.'

After passing through the shiny silver surface of the globe, they were briefly enclosed in darkness, before coming to rest in a small, green-lit lobby area.

A female official in a powder-blue uniform approached them. 'Chief Pundit? How can I help you?'

Pilo stumbled forwards as Sal shoved him from behind. 'I've been summoned by the Chronomaster,' he said, his voice higher than usual. 'He wants me to explain the foul-up just now in Sphere 12.'

The woman frowned, looking over his motley assortment of companions. 'And the others? What are they doing here?'

'They are here as part of the... the... uh... Topside Reintegration Programme. Have you not heard of it?'

'Enlighten me, Chief Pundit.' She didn't look convinced.

Pilo swallowed. Seeing that their escort had run out of inspiration, Raffi spoke up for him: 'The idea,' he extemporised, 'is to allow us Topsiders, that is the ones, like us, who are supporters of Secrocon, to become more aware of the inner workings of the Sphere, so to speak. The programme organisers thought that the more involved we feel in the whole process the better it'll be for our morale during the, er... on-going struggle against the Topside dissidents... and miscreants.'

'I see,' she blinked. 'Well I haven't heard of it.' She consulted her compad. 'The Chronomaster is busy right now. Some Seed Race Elect will shortly be having their final-phase meeting with him. Perhaps you'd all like to wait in Anteroom D at the end of that corridor.'

They began heading in the direction she indicated: Pilo in the lead, followed by Sal, Lastara, Raffi and Dario. The viridian lighting made everything shadowy and obscure, as if viewed underwater. Pilo looked uncertain about where to go.

Hesitantly, he pushed open the first door they came to. It was a store room filled with racks of white, close-fitting costumes. Like all official uniforms in the Chronosphere they had the rotating hourglass icon emblazoned above the left breast, but on this version, swirling around the symbol as if caught by a breeze, was a banner with the letters SR printed on it.

'Seed Race uniforms!' chirped Lastara. She smiled the way she always did when something she found amusing popped into her head. 'These could be your ticket into the Garden, Sal.'

'And yours,' replied Sal, with deadly seriousness. She walked into the room, then turned and faced them, her gun still pointing at Pilo. 'Okay, listen up. We're all going to become members of the Seed Race. We'll find the group of Seed Race Elect that are here for their meeting with the Chronomaster and mingle in with them so we're not noticed. Alright?'

Raffi was stunned at the audacity of the plan. And so, by the general silence that greeted her words, was everyone else.

'Alright?' repeated Sal, more urgently this time.

'I was joking, Sal,' said Lastara, her voice quavering.

'It's ridiculous,' pleaded Pilo. 'I'll be spotted immediately. I'm 24 for Bo's sake. Far too old.'

'You'll do as you're told, both of you. Now get changed.'

Five minutes later, they were all in costumes – the closest they could find to their different sizes – and back in the corridor. They were about to continue along it when they were arrested by a shout to their rear. 'Hey!' came the surprised yell. 'Where in hooly do you think you're going?' Raffi quickly pocketed his gun. A chill tightness gripped his insides as he turned. A blue-uniformed male was staring at them, face red from the heat of his agitation. 'You should be in Anteroom A,' he cried. 'Follow me. And be quick about it!' He spun on his heel and marched back up the corridor. They followed him back into the lobby and down another corridor. At the end of it, they found a congregation of about 15 young people, all in the same figure-hugging white uniforms.

'Phew! Just in time,' sighed the blue uniform. 'Don't wander off again now, will you. It's more than my job's worth. Right! I'll leave you kids to it.' As he marched away, Raffi looked cautiously around him at their fellow Seed Race Elect. They all wore relaxed, serene smiles, not dissimilar to Lastara's. They conversed quietly with each other, utterly incurious about the new arrivals. He noticed Sal discreetly checking out their faces, hoping against hope that Anna might be among them. He had done the same – and she wasn't. Then a crack of bright light appeared in the wall at the end of the corridor behind them, revealing itself to be a door. Calmly, the Elect filed through into the bright space beyond, turning alternately left and right as they entered. Raffi, Dario and Sal turned right – Pilo and Lastara went left. Raffi could see Sal wasn't happy about this, but there was nothing she could do without drawing attention to herself. Luckily, it looked as though Lastara was enjoying herself too much to blow the whistle on them just yet, and Pilo appeared so battered by recent events that he lacked the will to do much of anything except try to blend into the background.

The Elect stood on a narrow, transparent balcony that ran around the equator of a white-walled, spherical room. The room was some 20 metres in diameter and looked like a miniature version of Secrocon HQ, but without the bubbles and their interconnecting levitator tubes. This room was, in fact, entirely empty, apart from the Elect themselves and a black cube that hovered motionlessly some 10 metres from them in the exact centre of the room. This cube would have drawn attention to itself even if it hadn't been the only object in sight – there was something unnerving about its total and impenetrable blackness. Its surface didn't reflect the room's lighting, or anything at all. In fact there was nothing to suggest it even had a surface. Its box shape was only discernible from its silhouette, like a three-dimensional shadow. Then, very briefly, the cube faded, becoming almost a translucent grey. In those few seconds, Raffi thought he glimpsed something moving within it: pale green skin, the scaly side of a face, a pair of dark eyes that gleamed dimly like moonlight in inky black water. A knife-thin nose came into view, slightly hooked, with tiny flared nostrils. Below it stirred faintly moving lips, prominent, grey and snarling: almost lupine. Raffi was grateful when the cube's dark opacity was restored. The less he saw of such a face, the better.

'Seed Race Elect,' declared a voice from within the cube. It was the same high, sing-song voice Raffi had heard earlier on Pilo's wearable. 'Welcome! I speak to you here from the geometric centre of the Chronosphere. I am the Chronomaster, and this is the final phase of your initiation. Your minds and bodies have now been adjudged worthy of the life that awaits you as members of the Seed Race. From here, you will be taken to the Garden to live out your days in perfect happiness and tranquility.

'But before that, I want to spend a few minutes explaining to you the history of this great project of ours, so you can better understand the significance of the role you are about to play. My name – my real name – is Edo Carinae. I am a physicist by training. Together with my colleagues, Slim Trifid and Puppis Nova, I invented the Tricarno Subjective Time Dilator, the forerunner of the Chronosphere. The Tricarno was an amazing machine – a device that could literally speed up or slow down subjective time.

'I cannot describe to you the excitement of those early days. The machine we had created sped up our internal workings so that every second felt longer. We found whole new worlds inside those seconds – the beat of a hummingbird's wing, the tongue protraction of a rainforest frog. And beyond that, just waiting to be explored, were the superquick phenomena we were scarcely aware of: the life of rods, the motions of molecules and the explosions of miniature black holes. We were revolutionaries, overthrowing the auto-'ticktock'-cracy of clock-time; we were pioneers, colonising rich and fertile new temporal pastures; we were chrononauts, venturing into that vast, uncharted territory that lay between each tick of the clock, each blink of the eye and each beat of the heart.

'But there was a problem. Although there were no theoretical limits to the Tricarno's speed, we were limited by the human body. Its musculature, joints and skin weren't designed for these kinds of velocities. We experimented on lab-grown animals... and on ourselves. I managed to experience five hours within a second, but became sore and weak and had to lie down in a dark room for three days. We expended many years on the problem. Finally, I thought I had found a solution. I invented a special padded suit that I believed could cushion the body from the impact of superfast movements. But before we could be sure of its effectiveness, we had to test it...'

The white, spherical room faded away, and Raffi found himself standing inside a virtual laboratory, full of untidy wiring and machinery. A glass cube about four metres to a side dominated the room. Inside it was a tall, black, hourglass-shaped obelisk, similar to the one he'd seen earlier in Sphere 12, and a chair. Next to this cube stood a serious-looking young man with squinty eyes and juglike ears. He was assisting another man as he donned a thick, padded suit made of green shiny material. The man getting into the suit was facing away from Raffi, so he couldn't see his face.

'On the day of the test,' came the Chronomaster's voice, 'we were all in a state of high anticipation and nervousness. Naturally, as the suit's inventor, I volunteered to test it. My colleague, Slim Trifid, helped me into it while Puppis Nova manned the controls.'

Raffi watched the serious-looking man – Trifid – secure a spongy-looking green helmet with a visor over the other man's head. A door in the glass cube slid open and Edo Carinae – the future Chronomaster – entered and sat down on the chair. Puppis Nova was at a desk that sparkled with lights and buttons, his fingers poised over a lever.

'I persuaded them,' said Carinae, 'to take me up to 24 hours a second, twice as fast as any previous test on human or animal. Puppis and Slim were reluctant. As a precaution, they allowed me to experience only a millisecond at the maximum speed, equating to just over a minute of subjective time.'

The glass door slid closed. Nova pushed a lever slowly forwards and the hourglass started to glow. The seated figure of Carinae disappeared and then suddenly, instantaneously, reappeared lying on the floor of the cube. His body, twisted into an unnatural shape, was jerking uncontrollably. His suit looked dirty. The visor on his helmet was white with condensation. Nova hurriedly opened the door, then he and Trifid helped the figure out of the glass cube. They laid him on the floor and Trifid lifted the visor. He let out a cry of shock.

What had he seen? Raffi couldn't tell, because Trifid's body shielded him from the sight of the face inside the visor.

The laboratory vanished and they were back inside the white spherical room. Carinae spoke from inside his black cube: 'I was alive, but only just. I had been wrong about the suit. It hadn't protected me. I was hospitalised for the next few years: much of my body had to be rebuilt using artificial parts. I was now monstrous to look at, and despised the stares of nurses and visitors. I arranged for the lights to dim automatically whenever someone entered the room. Eventually I designed the darkness generator – this cube of lightlessness you see before you now. It does a good job of shielding me from your stares, and shielding you from the sight of me.

'Somehow, despite my terrible injuries, I clung onto life. And with every breath I could muster, I urged my colleagues to continue with the project. But after the accident, they could no longer find much enthusiasm for the work. For them, anyway, it had only ever been a scientific project. For me, it had always been something much, much more...

'In those dark days in hospital, I dreamed of creating a community of hundreds, if not thousands, all living at an unimaginable speed. My community would live in the world yet be unobservable to the people around us. We would be, quite literally, a world apart. I would construct my world from scratch, stripping it of all those miserable traits that have blighted human existence since the dawn of civilisation. Tyranny, corruption, cruelty and injustice would be replaced by liberty, fairness, kindness and equality. In my world, all needs would be catered for in abundance. People would eat delicious food, nourish their minds and souls with art and learning, and play to their heart's content. Freed from life's hardships, they would be able, at last, to discover their true potential as human beings: better, brighter, stronger and more virtuous. Fired by this vision, I gathered a new team of scientists around me. And slowly, over the next thirty years, the Chronosphere was built. My scientists found a new, revolutionary means of shielding the body from superfast speeds, not by using suits, but by altering the body itself. And, finally, and most importantly, we found the raw material, the Seed Race, for my community – you.

'And so, my friends, that is the story of the Chronosphere. And it gives me great pleasure that you will now be joining the community that I first dreamed of so many years ago in my hospital bed. I hope you enjoy your lives in the Garden and that, in time, you will all find compatible partners with whom to have children, so that the community can continue to flourish and grow. Go now, my young pioneers. You are ready to join the Seed Race!'

CHAPTER TWENTY-ONE

THE HEXAGONAL CHAMBER

affi, Sal, Dario, Lastara and Pilo had been last in, so they now found themselves at the front of the column that slowly filed out of the room. Back in the green-lit corridor, a blue-suited official smiled warmly at them and asked them to follow him. He led them back to the lobby area where more blue uniforms were awaiting them. One of them was the woman they had encountered on their arrival, but she didn't appear to recognise them. The Seed Race Elect were now split into five groups, each allocated to one of the blue uniforms. Raffi, Dario, Lastara and Sal found themselves forming one group. Pilo, looking almost paralysed with fear, was allocated to one of the other groups. The official in charge of Raffi's group marched them off down the curving corridor that led around the circumference of Sec HQ Central. After some thirty metres, when the curvature of the corridor had taken them fully out of sight of the lobby area, he stopped and turned. Raffi noticed that the official was pointing a gun at them. He felt strangely unsurprised by this – their luck was bound to run out sooner or later. Out of a doorway to their left came three more blue uniforms, all of them carrying guns aimed at the group. Finally, out of the same doorway emerged Avon Drak.

'Avon!' cried Lastara, running to him. 'Oh, Avon! They captured me. They made me take them here and wear this uniform!'

'Silence!' shouted Drak, pushing her away. 'Get back with your friends.'

'They're not my friends, Avon, I–'

'I said get back there!' His eyes, normally cool and grey, burned like hot coals. Lastara hastily rejoined the others.

'Disarm them,' instructed Avon, and a burly guard began removing the weapons that were making obvious bulges in their close-fitting pockets. Avon turned to one of the officials. 'Where's Metis?'

'He was allocated to another group, Chrono-Sensei.'

'Well bring him here.'

'Yes, Sir.' The official saluted and left.

Avon began pacing slowly up and down as he eyed each of his captives in turn. Finally, his attention rested on Lastara. 'What kind of a pitiful, third-rate operation are you running up there,' he thundered, 'that you let this rabble disarm your guard and then walk right out of there taking you with them? It makes me wonder what the hell I was thinking putting you in charge when you allow yourself to get kidnapped and your friends to cause complete mayhem all over Secrocon HQ for over two hours. I must have been out of my mind–'

'It was you who provided me with boys for guards!' Lastara shouted back. 'It's not my fault that they didn't act like men when they saw their queen in danger.'

Before Avon could respond to this, Pilo Metis appeared, still in his white uniform, escorted by two green-uniformed guards. 'Ah, Chief Pundit!' smiled Avon.

'I'm so sorry, Chrono-Sensei,' cried Pilo, falling to his knees before Drak. 'I tried my best. Honestly! I activated the alarm. But she…' He pointed a shaking finger at Sal. 'That girl was threatening me with extinction. I–I wouldn't have minded for myself. But my son… I couldn't bear the thought of…'

'Then you have no sense of proportion,' remarked Avon, still gazing warmly upon Pilo's pink, upturned face. 'What is a child's life next to our great project? How can you ever have thought of your individual desires at such a time? What is your boy's name?'

'Trey, Ch-Chrono-Sensei.'

Avon nodded, then drew a temp fi-er from his belt and placed the muzzle against Pilo's forehead.

'Well, Chief Pundit. You be-Treyed us. And, for that, Trey can no longer… be.'

'No!!!'

He pulled the trigger, blasting Pilo backwards at high speed. His body pulsed in and out of visibility for a second or two, then seemed to melt away into the floor.

Avon reholstered the gun and sauntered back to his captives. Raffi, with the Chief Pundit's final, horrified expression still branded on his memory, felt like he wanted to be sick. Sal's killing of the technician had been bad enough, but at least that had been an act borne of desperation. Drak's had been cold-blooded and – in Raffi's view – entirely unjustified: the man was clearly no traitor. He recalled the Chronomaster's description of the world he wished to create: tyranny, corruption, cruelty and injustice would be replaced by liberty, fairness, kindness and equality. The Chrono-Sensei did not appear to have signed up to that mission statement.

'Pilo Metis was lucky,' Avon said to them. 'He is now safely in the land of the never-was-and-never-will-be.' He looked at Raffi, Dario and Sal. 'Your fate will not be so pleasant. I will see you three again shortly in the Punishment and Experimentation Centre. Lastara, you come with me.' As she moved to join him, he murmured something to one of the guards, then turned and strode away down the corridor, Lastara scurrying along in his wake.

Raffi, Dario and Sal were led, at gunpoint, back to the lobby, which was now empty, and into a levitator. The light disc whisked them skywards, passing quickly through the bright sphere of Secrocon HQ and then into the long dark shaft that led back towards the Topside. The disc ceased its ascent before reaching the surface, however. They were led out of the shaft and down another featureless, anonymous corridor, through a doorway and into a large hexagonal chamber. Furnishing comprised of some metal seating that had been fixed to the floor alongside each wall. The only other exceptional feature of the room, apart from its shape, was its height: it soared some thirty or forty metres above them and, at the very top, horizontal bars of light shone through on all six sides.

Raffi went and sat down on one of the metal benches, placing his head in his hands. He felt emotionally stunned by all he had experienced since taking wing with the Suicide Squad three and a half hours earlier.

'Here we are then,' he heard Dario growl at Sal. 'Exactly where we would have been if you hadn't tried your crazy stunt. Only now we've made that bloke mad as a cut snake and instead of offering us a spot of light re-education as he planned to, he'll probably kill us. That's the sum total of your achievements this afternoon, Sal. Oh yeah, not to mention the death of an innocent man!'

Sal didn't reply. Raffi only heard her footsteps pacing the floor of the chamber, maybe looking for a means of escape. Eventually, he heard her say: 'I didn't realise the gun's setting had reverted to "kill". I was trying to time-loop the guy, like I did the guards earlier.'

'Taking a bit of a chance, weren't you?'

'Perhaps you've forgotten how desperate our situation was at that moment, what with fighter-droids pouring in on all sides! I'll make it up somehow,' she added quietly. 'I'll find his next of kin and compensate them in some way.'

'A worthy thought, but totally unnecessary,' came a voice from behind Raffi. He leapt up and twirled around. The wall he'd just been leaning against – one of the six sides of the room – had become transparent. Behind it he saw a densely equipped control room. Grey-uniformed technicians sat before workstations, pressing buttons, flicking switches and observing screens. Avon stood in the middle of the room, flanked by two green-uniformed guards. He was smiling warmly at Sal. 'My dear girl, the next of kin of Statisticon Cy Vesta, the man you despatched into nonpersonhood, will soon be completely unaware he ever existed. The temp fi-er saw to that. It doesn't just erase old family holoscans, but people's memories as well.'

Raffi discovered it was true. He found he had virtually no recollection now of the man Sal had killed. Even Pilo Metis had started to fade as a distinct character in his memory.

'I shall miss young Cy, however,' continued Avon, 'at least for the short time I continue to remember him. For he was one of the two hundred personally loyal to me. The Chief Pundit was not among them. He was much more dispensable. Like most at Secrocon HQ, he still firmly believed in Carinae's fantasy of a world of endless love and peace. It's a folly, of course, a romantic delusion.

'But why am I telling you this?... Because you're going to be dead very soon, that's why, and I would hate you to die thinking that dreary old fool Carinae will get his way and we'll all soon be going around in sandals with daisies in our hair singing songs of love on our glitterstrings. I'm not saying the Chronomaster isn't a great man. It was his vision, his drive, that created the Chronosphere. But now he's an *old* man, and he can't face the fact that his ultimate goal, his longed-for paradise on earth, is unattainable. Human nature simply isn't like that. Where you have community, you have conflict, inequality and injustice. These are not evils to be banished, they're inevitable consequences of who we are. Even in a group like the Seed Race, specially selected for their beauty and their brains, there will be those who are more beautiful or more intelligent than others, and they'll thrive, while their rivals fail. That's simply the way things are.

'My followers and I recognise this, and we're working to create a different kind of world here in the Chronosphere, a world of rules and discipline in which people know their place. Human beings are always happier, after all, when they know their place. For some chrono-years now I've been building up a secret powerbase. I have followers in Secrocon Police, in the Re-Ed Centre, at Secrocon HQ and, of course, here in my own private fiefdom, which Carinae knows nothing about – the Punishment and Experimentation Centre. We're almost ready to stage our takeover of the Chronosphere. Phase One was our sabotage of the cooling plant and technical control centre, which caused the heat to rise and the service quality to fall on the Topside. Phase Two was the Malfunction, trapping people within the Sphere. Phase Three was the inevitable consequence of the first two phases: the breakdown of law and order and the emergence of territorial tribes. Through the naïve and wonderful Lastara Blue – who still believes I'm working for Carinae – I took over the strongest tribe, putting me in effective control of the Topside. All this is having the intended effect. The technocrats, the re-educators, police and security forces – the people who run the Sphere – are starting to panic.

They're losing faith in Carinae and his idea that a world without rules can ever be possible. In that sense, the Topside is now the evil twin of the Garden – or a prediction of how it might ultimately turn out. People are looking for someone strong to restore order and that someone will be me. My followers are in place. They know what they have to do. In a matter of days, I'll be installed in the silver sphere of Sec HQ Central as the new Chronomaster.'

Raffi struggled to take this all in. So the whole collapse of the Topside, from the bad food and the heat to the Malfunction and all the chaos and death that followed was Drak's doing. It wasn't a technical failure, but a deliberate and cynical bid for power by this man. And the Chronomaster knew nothing about it!

Drak continued: 'Sadly my friends, you won't be around to witness my little coup. You'll be long dead by then. And as a special treat before you die, I want you to experience some of the fascinating things we've learned through our experiments on Re-Ed Centre inmates. Carinae promised you a beautiful life. The best I can offer you is an interesting death.' Avon nodded to one of the technicians at the workstation in front of him and the man pushed a lever. Pink light flooded the room. Raffi felt no different. He looked around him, trying to work out what had changed. He saw Sal behind him, starting to look up towards something above them, and Dario moving his hand to his head as though about to scratch it in puzzlement. Then, suddenly, he was facing front again, watching the man push the lever forwards and seeing the light pinkening around them. Without meaning to, he found himself looking behind, just as he'd done seconds before. And there was Sal, craning her head upwards just like previously, while Dario repeated the raising of his hand. Facing front once more, he watched frustratedly as the lever moved forward and the pink light descended. Like a preprogrammed automaton, he felt himself rotate in time to see Sal's face and then Dario's arm rising on their preordained paths. On the fifth or sixth of these loops, Raffi attempted to apply some logic to his situation: the loop obviously wasn't all-encompassing or he wouldn't be aware of it: his consciousness had to be outside the loop, or else how could he observe it? So if his consciousness was outside it, then maybe it could will his body to break out of it, too. On the next loop – the seventh or was it eighth? – he deliberately tried not to turn, and found that, with an effort of will, he could. Several loops after that, he geared himself up to try something more radical. As soon as he was facing front again, even before the pink light suffused the room, he forced himself to make a mad and sudden dash across the room towards where Dario was standing. He managed about half the distance before finding himself facing the transparent window once more. Raffi tried several more such dashes over the next few minutes, but gradually, as the loops continued inexorably to shackle him, he grew tired and his mind became dull. In the end it was much easier to simply go where his body wanted to take him. He didn't know how long it continued, but by the time the pink light finally faded, he felt completely numb and weak and was scarcely able to think. That, his crumbling mind told him, was torture – more shattering, more soul-destroying than anything he had felt before.

'One more before I despatch you for good,' smiled Avon to his dazed captors. 'This one is my special favourite. I call it Zeno Space, after that wonderful ancient Greek purveyor of paradoxes, Zeno of Elea. He suggested that if Achilles and a tortoise have a race, and the tortoise is given a head start of, say, 100 metres, then Achilles will never be able to catch the tortoise, no matter how fast he runs or how slow the tortoise crawls. Why should that be? Because by the time Achilles has completed the 100 metres, the tortoise would have moved on by another metre, and by the time Achilles has run that additional metre, the tortoise would have moved on another centimetre, and by the time Achilles has run that centimetre, the tortoise would have moved on another millimetre, and so on, into endlessly tiny fractions... Now, we all know that this is not how the world works in reality. The story's assumption that space and time, like numbers, are infinitely divisible, is simply untrue. Untrue in this world at least. Not so in Zeno Space. In Zeno Space, space and time *are* infinitely divisible. In Zeno Space, you are Achilles, always closing in on that tortoise, but never quite reaching it.' Avon nodded to a technician and a blue-tinted light descended on the chamber.

Raffi blinked, and then blinked again. He couldn't believe that Anna Morrow now stood before him. Dressed in a lovely blue gown, her head tilted slightly towards the floor, she gazed demurely upwards at him. At his answering look of happy recognition, her brown eyes widened, and her lips of the ripest cherry broke into a smile of bright and increasing confidence. She looked more ravishing than he could ever remember. As she stepped towards him, she sighed: 'Raphael, my angel. You came back for me! I knew you would.' She came closer and he looked forward to the brush of her fingers on his hands, this time without the burn that had marred their first encounter – the excruciating pain caused by touching a person who is travelling in the opposite temporal direction to oneself. He saw the pulse of excitement in her slim, pale neck, the warmth rising in her cheeks, echoing the changes in his own body as he anticipated the press of hers against his and the first glorious kiss. Closer and closer she came. He ached for her. His breath came in urgent, ragged sighs. When would they finally touch? Why did these final seconds drag themselves out so? He saw the bewilderment that clouded her eyes and knew she was enduring the same frustration.

Time had slowed – for their bodies at least. They were but centimetres away, yet it might have been light years for the impossibility of bridging that gap. They were still moving towards each other, but by ever-tinier fractions of millimetres, until the movement felt like no movement at all. They stared at each other across the tiny yet limitless abyss, physically tensed and ready for the embrace they both desired more than anything, yet at the same time sad and resigned to the fact that they never would experience it.

How long did they stand there facing each other? Mountains rose and fell, ice caps spread and receded. Whole continents vanished beneath the ocean swell. Or so it seemed. At last, the blue light faded. And, to Raffi's great relief, Anna was gone. Exhausted and utterly spent, he sank to the floor, and Drak's voice came gently to his ears: 'I've had this idea for a spectacular style of death and I've been longing for a chance to try it out.' Raffi raised his eyes to the transparent wall and saw Avon chuckle to himself. 'This is going to be just perfect,' said the chrono-sensei. 'We're going to dilate you to one second per second, then raise you to the ravenous mob above. That's right! This room rises directly into the Lower Atrium of Time Tower, where the residents haven't had a decent meal for... ooh... two weeks? They're probably ready to turn cannibal around now. And, as you'll be dilated, it should feel something like being lowered into a lake of million-mile-an-hour piranha. You'll be stripped to the bone before you even know what's hit you.' He raised his hand in a farewell salute. 'Good-bye Raffi, Dario and Sal. Bon voyage.' He looked like an amiable neighbour wishing them a pleasant holiday. Then he raised his head to the roof high above: 'Bon appetit,' he murmured to whoever might be listening up there.

A button was pressed in the control room and Raffi felt the hiss and vibration of hydraulics beneath them as the entire floor of the chamber – which he now saw was separate from the walls – began to rise. At the same time, Drak and everyone else in the office beyond the partition began to move with increasing speed, flying about the place like a mass of spiders. Soon all human life in the control room became a blur, a mere flicker in the air, and only the furniture and equipment remained visible.

The floor of the chamber rose quickly, as did the roof above them, and the light of the Lower Atrium flooded the chamber. No longer welcome, that light spelt only death. Dario, still dazed after the tortures, blundered around trying to find something, anything, to jam in the crack between walls and floor to try to halt or slow their ascent. He tried to rip a metal bench from its floor bolts but it wouldn't be budged and, as the floor continued its inexorable climb, he eventually gave up. Raffi summoned up the energy to rise to his feet. Instinctively, the three of them moved towards the middle of the room.

'Hold my hands,' Sal told them. 'Let's stand in a circle – facing outwards. Keep your eyes open. Let's not be scared. We'll face whatever comes with our eyes open.'

Raffi couldn't help the sob of fear in his chest, but he obeyed her. Dario did too, completing the circle.

'Let's not be scared,' Sal repeated. The floor was now just a few metres short of the surface and already the features of the Lower Atrium were coming into view. 'When they come, it'll be very quick, I promise.'

'Good-bye, Sal. Good-bye Raffi,' cried Dario. 'I love you both.'

CHAPTER TWENTY-TWO

⧗

AND WHERE DO YOUR LOYALTIES LIE?

The floor slowed its ascent, then stopped. They were just half a metre below the surface, effectively in a shallow hexagonal crater, easily accessed by anyone on the Lower Atrium of Time Tower. Raffi scarcely recognised the place: the shops and restaurants were now heaps of rubble and scorched and twisted girders. There was a strong stench of decay. No one was around – no one he could see, anyway. How soon before someone decided to take a bite out of him or just hack him to bits for the hell of it? He braced himself for the pain. At least when it happened it would be quick – hopefully too quick to even register as a conscious experience. One millisecond here, the next – dead. That, surely, wasn't a bad way to go! Surprisingly he found, after more seconds had ticked peacefully by, that he was still alive. Why the delay when every passing second spelt days up here? Now he was confused as well as frightened. On either side of him, Sal's and Dario's hands tightly clenched his own, their sweat mingling with his. No one breathed.

They heard a noise. It sounded like a deep groan. The floor beneath them vibrated, then began, very slowly, to sink. They were heading back down. Sal was the first to start moving again. She broke away from them and ran to the edge of the floor to see what was happening through the glass partition, which was just now starting to come into view. 'Quickly,' she cried. 'Come and look.'

Raffi and Dario dashed over and looked down at the control room. Avon, the guards and the technicians had all collapsed on the floor. And there, at the workstation controls stood a small, thin, blond boy – a boy Raffi had never expected to see again.

'Jonah!' Dario, Raffi and Sal shouted his name almost in unison. Jonah looked up and briefly nodded to them. He waited for the hexagonal floor to realign itself with the control room floor, then pressed a button on the console. The glass partition slid upwards.

Raffi was the first out of the chamber and the first to hug Jonah. Dario was hot on his heels. 'Jonah! I can't believe you're okay!' Raffi had questions – too many questions. And around him the guards, and Avon Drak, were already starting to stir.

'Quick!' said Sal. 'Let's get out of here!' They raced out of the door at the back of the control room and down the corridor towards a bank of levitators. The four of them leapt onto a light disc and Sal pressed the bottom-most key on the levitator's long panel: Sec HQ Central.

'What's Sec HQ Central?' asked Jonah.

'No time to explain,' she answered. 'But it's the only means of accessing the Garden.'

'What's the Garden?'

'I think it's where I'll find my sister.'

'How are we supposed to do it, Sal?' asked Raffi. 'The first time we might have fooled them. But they're on the alert now. They'll recognise us for sure.'

'We'll manage it,' replied Sal. 'I don't know how, but we will.'

Raffi thought Sal was being wildly optimistic. Then again, ten minutes ago he'd have found the idea of them still being alive right now wildly optimistic, so you just never knew.

'How in hooly did you overpower Drak and all his guards, Jonah?' asked Dario.

'Easy,' said Jonah. 'I used a hyperbaric dilator to apply a temporal compression pocket to the entire control room, slowing it down to about 120 days to a second – that's 20 times slower than normal chronospheric time. So you lot appeared to slow down to their eyes, just as they'd expect. And I guess they must have looked speeded up to you. In fact, you remained in normal C-time, which is why you didn't become a picnic for the cannibals up there. Then I switched off the compression pocket, giving them a massive jolt of temporal whiplash – that's why they all lost consciousness.'

'Brilliant work, mate!' said Dario, clapping him on the back.

Raffi shook his head in awe at the little genius.

'One day,' said Sal. 'Not now, but one day, you're going to have to explain to us how you happened to be hanging around outside that particular control room at that particular moment with a hyperbaric dilator?'

'It's okay,' said Jonah. 'It's not a long story. My biker, a guy named Scram, crash-landed in Austra Bella territory and we were immediately captured and taken to her holoplex HQ. Queen Bella wasn't around and we were left waiting there for a while until Avon Drak showed up and sent us down to the PEC. The guards weren't watching us too closely and we gave them the slip. They chased us and Scram was hit unfortunately. I got away and hid out in this equipment room, which is where I spotted the hyperbaric dilator. On the other side of the wall was the control room and I was able to listen in while Drak was torturing you guys. I wish I could have done something to help, but I was all out of ideas. Then, when he said he was going to dilate you, the idea came to me.'

The light disc flashed into the bright white vista of Secrocon HQ and Jonah gave a low whistle of astonishment.

'Jonah,' began Raffi. 'We should tell you that...'

'Queen Bella,' continued Dario, 'is actually...'

'Lastara,' finished Sal.

Jonah stared at them. 'Where is she now?'

'We don't know,' said Raffi. 'She's loyal to Drak, I'm afraid. He's the Secrocon contact she was always talking about. She was with us when he captured us at Sec HQ. We don't know where he took her.'

This time, the disc flew right on through Sphere 12 without stopping. It plunged into the top of the chrome ball of Sec HQ Central, then slowed to a stop.

'What now?' asked Dario.

'I don't know,' said Sal. 'Just use your wits and, if necessary, your fists.'

As the glass partition opened, Raffi saw a figure in blue emerging from one of the corridors. 'Quick!' he whispered, beckoning them to follow him into the green-hued shadows on the far side of the lobby. As the blue-suited figure passed them, Raffi leapt out and grabbed him by the neck, clapping his hand over the official's mouth before he could scream. He dragged him back to the corner where the others were crouching. Dario took the gun from the man's belt and held it to his head. 'You have to get us into the Garden, mate!' he whispered.

The man shook his head, eyes wide with alarm. He was mumbling something from beneath Raffi's hand.

'Don't scream now!' warned Raffi. 'Or my friend here will kill you.' He slowly removed his hand.

'I can't help you,' cried the man.

'Shhh!' said Raffi. 'Whatever you say, say it softly.'

'Why do you want to get into the Garden?' the man whimpered.

Dario smiled. 'What's your name, sport?'

'Herkel Slipher.'

'Do you know anything about the Chrono-Sensei's secret plan to take over the Chronosphere, Herkel?'

The man paled. He began to shake. 'I... I've heard rumours, but...'

'And where do your loyalties lie?'

'With... with... They lie in the same direction as yours,' he moaned, his eyeballs fixed shakily on the gun muzzle.

Dario chuckled. 'In that case, you'll know we're planning on making our move against the Chronomaster tonight. You know that, don't you?'

The man gulped and nodded. 'Of course! Of course!'

'And you'll also know that everyone has to get into position so we can make a coordinated attack. We've got our people Topside and in Sec HQ and in Re-Ed and in PEC. The only place we haven't yet infiltrated is the Garden. And that's where you come in, Herkel, my friend. You have to get us in there. If you can manage it, I'll make sure I mention it to the Chrono-Sensei and I'm sure you'll be appropriately rewarded. But if you refuse to help us, well, I can't vouch for what'll happen to you.'

⧗

A minute later, Herkel Slipher was leading them along the corridor they'd been sent down earlier that day. In the store room they found a white uniform for Jonah, who quickly changed into it. Herkel then led them to another levitator. The shaft of this one was not transparent, but milk-white. 'This leads to the Garden,' he informed them. 'There are always two people guarding the entrance. They're completely loyal to the Chronomaster. I don't know what I'll say to them.'

'Just tell them we're part of the group of Seed Race Elect that went in there an hour ago,' said Sal. 'We were delayed, that's all.'

The man gulped again, and nodded.

After another long descent, the levitator doors opened on a lobby area. At the far end was a set of very ordinary grey metal doors. Two green-uniformed guards stood in front of them.

Herkel Slipher led the way.

'Who's this lot then?' asked one of the guards lazily. He didn't seem perturbed by their approach. 'We weren't expecting another batch today.'

'They're part of the earlier group,' stammered Slipher. 'Delayed.' The man was sweating. Raffi was sure his nervousness would make the guards suspicious. They looked them over like farmers inspecting a herd of sheep. 'Biometric card, please,' demanded the other guard. Herkel handed it over. The guard looked it over, then passed it back. He pressed his finger to a scanpad next to the door and a thin sheet of light shone between the metal doors. This wasn't like electric light though. It had a hazy, golden quality, like late afternoon summer sunshine.

CHAPTER TWENTY-THREE

THE WHITE TOWER

carpet of lush green grass lapped the other side of the metal doors. It spread outwards from there like a perfect lawn, rising in a gentle gradient. Sal, Dario and Jonah stepped over the steel threshold and onto the soft and yielding turf. As Raffi followed them, a cool breeze of beautiful, fresh-smelling air caught his nostrils. Sal immediately raced ahead. The three boys jogged at a more leisurely pace up the short rise to the summit of a hillock. The view that opened up beneath them was like a vision of heaven. Stretched out on all sides as far as Raffi could see, melting into a greenish blue horizon, undulating lawns of the freshest, greenest, newly cut grass, shady hollows and gentle hillocks, small willows drooping over limpid pools, streams that shone like polished glass over glossy white and grey rocks. Dotted around this landscape were hundreds of young people, all dressed in identical white uniforms. Yet despite their great number, there was no sense of overcrowding: the dimensions of the Garden were so enormous, it could easily

have accommodated many more. Some of the boys and girls were in groups, some alone, some walking, others standing, talking or just daydreaming. One group was enjoying a picnic. The food looked fresh and abundant. Another lot were swimming and splashing around in a sunlit rock pool.

But how, wondered Raffi, could this endless vista be accommodated within the confines of the Chronosphere? Big as it was, this seemed on a different order of magnitude. He looked behind him towards the metal doors they had just come through, and was surprised to see nothing but more endless grass. Had the doorway simply materialised in the middle of a field? But then, looking more closely, he discerned the faint outline of a door in the air, and he began to see that he'd been fooled by a simple optical trick. The field of grass was only partly real. At a certain point no more than 20 or so metres back from the summit of the hillock where he stood, the field faded into a painted backdrop of the same hue. They were, in fact, bounded on all sides by a circular wall of greenish grey, fading to pale sky blue. The wall formed a shallow rise, like the edge of a bowl, never reaching vertical – it was, undoubtedly, the inner side of the Chronosphere's base, and it had been painted in a way to make it look like a far-distant horizon.

'There's Sal,' said Jonah. Raffi turned back to the valley below them and followed the line of Jonah's finger. Sal's bright blue hair was unmistakable. She was running from group to group, no doubt asking them if they'd seen her sister. The three of them raced off after her, leaping over small bushes and narrow streams. Raffi enjoyed the feel and smell of fresh air and the sun on his face. Artificial or not, it felt like the real thing. The sky above them was a painting, much like the roof of the Topside, but it seemed far enough away not to impede the sense of being outside.

When they caught up with her, Sal was interrogating a group of girls. 'Her name is Anna,' she told them. 'She's got dark hair. Pretty face. She may be behaving a bit strangely. Are you sure you haven't seen her?'

The girls didn't seem to be listening, or were simply not interested in what she was saying.

'How did they let you in here?' one of them asked, a hint of distaste on her attractive face. 'I don't mean to be rude, but you're not very pretty. And as for that hair!' She broke down in giggles, which prompted the other girls to start giggling, too.

'They must really be scraping the barrel,' sniggered one girl.

'She'll never find a partner,' guffawed another.

Dario, outraged to hear these remarks, strode up to them and put his arm around Sal's shoulder. Raffi saw the surprise in their faces as they registered Dario's face and physique in such affectionate proximity to the object of their mockery. 'Now listen up, ladies,' he declared. 'Sal here happens to be my girlfriend, and any insult to her is an insult to me. So just watch what you're saying.'

Sal shrugged away his arm. She clearly would have preferred to face down the insults herself without any help from Dario. Raffi saw the hurt in his friend's warm brown eyes at this rejection of his attempt at gallantry.

'I just want to know if you've seen my sister,' persisted Sal.

No one spoke. They looked back at her with the typical blank-eyed stare of wealthy Island City girls. Eventually one of the group said: 'Anyone fancy a swim? The water's gorgeous.' This suggestion brought the group back to life.

'Yeah! Let me just get my towel.'

'You bet. I'm there.'

'Race you!'

'Last one's a loser!'

They ran off, their voices and giggles ringing in the air like the twitterings of tropical birds.

'Fat lot of good they were,' said Dario.

'So much for Edo Carinae's promise of "better, brighter and more virtuous"!' added Raffi.

'Good point, mate. Did they really select these kids for their intelligence?'

'That was the Chronomaster's plan. Drak wanted willing followers for his police state. Looks like the Chrono-Sensei got his way.'

'Speaking of Drak,' butted in Jonah, 'As soon as he comes to his senses, he'll be sending an army of fighter droids after us. Our best hope is to split up. That way we'll also have more chance of finding Sal's sister.'

'I don't like the idea of separating,' said Dario.

'Any better suggestions?'

'No.'

'Where's Sal?' interrupted Raffi.

They turned to see Sal striding off again, this time towards a white tower that rose up out of a small valley about 300 metres from where they stood. Raffi was surprised he hadn't noticed such an arresting structure before. It looked like the turret of a fairytale castle: tall, white and perfectly round, with a gracefully curving outline rising from a wide base to a slender pinnacle. Crenellated parapets projected from the tower at regular intervals and it was topped by a conical red steeple that was high enough to seem almost to blend with the sky.

Once again, the boys had to break into a jog to catch up with Sal. As they approached the tower they saw young men and women entering and leaving through a wooden door at its base. A few were also visible peering over the parapets or leaning out of the arched windows that dotted the pure white stone wall. The Seed Race barely glanced at the newcomers as they passed among them.

They entered the shadowy interior of the tower. A stone staircase spiralled up the inner wall, disappearing through a gap in the wood-beamed ceiling a few metres above their heads. Sal took the stairs two at a time, barging past a descending group of boys and causing them to glare and mutter in annoyance. Raffi, Dario and Jonah followed at a more leisurely pace. The first floor looked like a communal dining hall, with long tables laid with eating implements and drinking vessels. Further up, the floors contained rows of beds. Jonah struggled to keep up with the others and was about two floors below them when Sal finally stopped – on floor eight. A group of five boys and girls were sitting on their beds, playing 'Alien Encounters' on their wearables. Another boy was leaning out of the window, enjoying the view.

'I'm looking for Anna Morrow,' said Sal breathlessly. 'Have any of you seen her?'

Reluctantly they raised their eyes to her, seemingly irritated by this stranger who had disturbed their game.

'Who are you?' asked a large girl with freckles on her nose.

'I'm Anna's sister. One of you must have seen her. Dark hair, dark eyes. Pretty face. She might be something of a loner.'

They looked at her for a while, then turned their attention back to their wrist consoles. 'You don't look like you belong here,' commented a small, round-faced boy.

'You should go,' said a girl with blonde ringlets.

'Zapped you, Jem!' exclaimed a girl with prominent front teeth.

'You evil witch!' whined a tall boy with long frizzy hair.

'Look, I'm sick of this,' shouted Sal. She ran up to the nearest one – the small, round-faced boy – and shook him violently. 'Why won't any of you answer my question?'

The boy looked shocked and dazed. Freckles got off her bed and shoved Sal in the chest, making her stagger backwards. 'How dare you?' she said.

'Apologise to him,' said blonde ringlets.

'Shall I call Secrocon?' asked prominent front teeth.

'It's alright, Secrocon are coming,' said the boy at the window. 'Come and see.'

They all clustered around him. Raffi went to another window at the far end of the room and witnessed a swarm of armoured fighter-droids charging across the grass, converging on the tower.

'There are about fifty of them approaching on this side,' he told the others. 'They'll be here any minute.'

Dario stared over the heads of the Seed Race kids. 'We've got the same number coming at us from this direction. Looks like we're done for, mate.'

Raffi looked around, searching for some means of defence. 'These beds,' he said. 'They could form a useful barricade.' He tried picking one up. It had a heavy metal frame and was a struggle to lift. 'Or maybe they could be a kind of weapon... Jonah, Dario. Help me, will you?'

⧗

'Hey! Ow!' The big, freckle-faced girl who had shoved Sal in the chest was now nursing a red mark on her cheek. Sal struck her again, this time on the other cheek, then pushed her backwards onto the floor. The girl began to cry.

'Now listen,' said Sal. 'One of you's going to tell me what you know right now, or else I'll just keep hitting her, okay?'

The others backed away from her, looking shocked and cowed by this violent demonstration.

⧗

While Sal confronted the floor-eighters near the window, the boys began piling up beds on the landing at the top of the spiral staircase. Raffi's plan was to wait for the droids to start mounting the stairway below, then to launch a bed down the steps. With sufficient momentum, one bed was probably heavy enough to knock half a dozen droids off their feet. Raffi had no idea how many floors there were above them, but if they all contained beds like this one, they should have enough to make quite an effective defence. Dario performed a test run, pushing a bed down the steps. It performed better than expected, bouncing downwards with impressive speed and momentum before crashing onto the landing below. 'I wouldn't want to be coming up while that thing's coming down,' he said.

⧗

'We don't know anything,' said the buck-toothed girl. 'Now leave her alone, will you.'

Sal marched up to her and raised her hand to strike her, before letting it drop limply to her side.

Raffi thought she looked tired. With Sal he always had the feeling that she knew what to do next. But he didn't get that feeling now.

'Secrocon'll be here any minute,' said the boy by the window. 'Then you lot will be in big troub... Hey what've you done with our beds. Put them back.'

'Sit down!' shouted Sal. 'All of you! Sit down and face the wall. If any of you so much as moves, I'm going to throw you out of the window.'

Scowling, they obeyed.

⧗

Raffi moved to the vacated window. The first droids had reached the base of the tower and were now streaming through the doorway. Far below, he could hear the distant clatter of boots on stone steps.

'Okay,' he said. 'They'll be here any minute now. You guys get ready. I'll check out the bed situation upstairs, in case we have to make a tactical withdrawal.'

He raced up the steps, three at a time. The dormitory above also contained ten beds. It was empty except for one, a red-haired girl with green eyes and a pale, heart-shaped face. Her appearance stirred faint memories in Raffi. She was sitting on her bed in the furthest corner, knees close together, very scared.

'What's going on?' she asked.

'Don't worry,' said Raffi. 'We don't want to hurt you.'

'I heard your friend,' said the girl. 'The one who's looking for her sister.'

'What about it?' Raffi was impatient to get back downstairs to help Jonah and Dario.

'I think I've met her. I don't know her name, but there is a strange girl who lives on her own at the very top of the tower. She's very pretty. I've spoken to her a few times. She says she used to be older. But that doesn't make any sense. Does it?'

A shiver ruffled the hairs on Raffi's neck when he heard this. 'Yes,' he said. 'That makes a lot of sense. Listen, I've got to go back downstairs now. Will you do me a favour? Will you go upstairs and ask that girl to come down to the eighth floor. Tell her her sister is here. Will you do that?'

The redhead nodded.

'Thanks,' said Raffi. Suddenly, he remembered where he'd seen her before. He smiled at her. 'Are you happy in this place?'

She looked at him as if puzzled by the question. 'Of course I am.'

'Do you want to go home?'

'This is my home.'

'Your name is Mira, isn't it? Mira Chailin.'

'How did you know?'

'I saw you the day you were kidnapped. On Tomorrow and Third.'

'You mean the day I was selected for Re-Ed.'

He nodded. 'Don't you miss your life before then? When you were free?'

'I *am* free,' she said.

Raffi sensed an unreconstructed humanity behind her words: some part of her the indoctrinators hadn't been able to reach. But there was no time now to probe further. 'Please get Anna for us,' he said, before running back down the stairs.

The fighter-droids' footsteps were now as loud and urgent as an approaching storm.

'Get to your stations,' cried Dario. 'They'll be here any second now. He and Jonah held the first bed in position at the top of the staircase.

Raffi lay on his belly and peered down over the edge of the gap where the staircase emerged onto their floor. From here he could see part of the floor and most of the staircase directly below. 'Okay, when I say "drop", you two let go of the bed,' he told them.

The first gleaming armoured figures emerged on the landing of Floor Seven. Their metal faces were only rudimentarily human, with slit mouths and black holes for eyes. These droids were built for brute action and had none of the usual refinements found on service or companion robots. They immediately began mounting the flight that led to Floor Eight.

'Wait for it,' said Raffi. He wanted to leave the launch until the last possible moment to maximise its impact – after this one, they would lose the element of surprise. 'Wait for it!' There were now a dozen droids on the staircase.

'Hey, Raffi, they're nearly on us,' yelled Jonah, who had a better view than Dario. 'We should drop it now!'

'Wait for it,' repeated Raffi, who wanted at least twenty on the staircase before they let go of the bed. Then he saw that the first droids were just ten or so steps from the top and that time had run out. 'Okay, drop!' he shouted.

The bed began its tumble and bump down the steps, and a ripple of agitation ran through the droids immediately below: red lights began to flash in their foreheads, a clear sign of alarm. But the bed had only started to gather its momentum when the first droids put out their metal clamper-hands to stop it. With vigorous surges of auxiliary power, released from other parts of their bodies, they managed to halt the bed in its tracks and prevent a catastrophic domino collapse through their ranks. Raffi watched incredulous as, with a triumphant roar of waste gases, exhaled through their slit mouths and nostrils, the androids recommenced their climb, pushing the bed before them, back up towards the top of the stairs.

⌛

CHAPTER TWENTY-FOUR

THIS IS WHERE WE STAND AND FIGHT

Seeing what was happening, Dario flew into action, running down the steps at full tilt and throwing himself against the top end of the bed. His weight and momentum, together with gravity, was enough to halt the droids in their tracks, but not quite enough to send them into reverse. With more of them gathering at the bottom of the stairwell, the teetering equilibrium would soon turn in the machines' favour. Jonah and Raffi, seeing this, immediately ran to give Dario support. Their contribution was enough to turn the tide. Slowly at first, the bed began to move downwards, and this time there was no stopping it. Raffi saw the flashing alarm signals in the faces of the droids below him, squashed up against the metal-framed bedstead, as they fell backwards into the crowd of warrior-droids coming up behind them. He could almost hear screams bursting from their slit mouths, but that was probably his euphoric imagination. The bed did its work, although worse news than the bed for the droids nearer the bottom was the crushing weight of robots falling on them from above. In all, more than twenty droids were deposited in a smoking, broken heap on Floor Seven. But the boys had no time to celebrate, as more of the killer dolls were already surging up from Floor Six, clambering over their fallen comrades and mounting the staircase with frightening speed.

'Quick,' yelled Dario. 'Another bed.'

He and Raffi raised the next bed into position and launched it before waiting for the word from Jonah, who had now replaced Raffi on lookout. The bed clattered down the steep curve of the stairway, knocking half a dozen more droids off their feet and pushing them down to join the growing pile below.

Still the droids came: a third contingent arrived, and then a fourth, each one running smack into a heavy metal missile launched from the floor above. Watching the carnage, Raffi wondered about the mentality of these machines. Did their programming not allow them to think strategically, or was their strategy simply one of individual self-sacrifice in the knowledge that their sheer numbers would eventually overwhelm the enemy?

They had been fighting for no more than fifteen minutes – or so it seemed – and already they were down to just two beds. Raffi turned to Sal. He hadn't yet had a chance to tell her about his encounter with Mira. 'It's time we went upstairs,' he told her.

She nodded.

'One more after that one, you guys,' Raffi told Jonah and Dario, then get up to the next floor as fast as you can. Sal and I will start preparing the beds up there.

Jonah raised his thumb to show he'd heard, then turned back in time to help Dario launch the penultimate bed.

Raffi followed Sal up the steps to Floor Nine. He was halfway there when he noticed that the Floor-Eighters, still sitting facing the wall, were now talking urgently with each other. Suddenly they got up and, as a group, ran over to where Jonah and Dario were placing the final bed into position. Before Jonah was even aware of them, he was pushed headlong down the stairs. He fell heavily down six or seven steps before landing in a dazed heap with his back and head against the wall. Raffi heard the blast of an energy projectile and Jonah screamed, clutching his side. Dario raced down a few steps and, using the temp fi-er he'd taken from Herkel Slipher, erased the droid sniper before it could get off another round. The Floor-Eighters, startled by the gunfire, raced back to the far side of the room. Dario approached Jonah, firing blindly below him as he did so, then hoisted Jonah over his shoulder, ignoring his yells of pain. Dario had almost made it back to the top of the steps when a laser projectile hit him in the calf. He recoiled and half collapsed against the wall. Somehow he managed to hop and stumble up the final steps before dropping Jonah on the floor.

'Jeebus!' he cried, then collapsed.

Raffi pocketed the gun Dario had dropped, then lifted Jonah, who was surprisingly light, and hoisted him over his shoulder. He started up the steps to Floor Nine. 'Dario,' he screamed. 'You've got to get up the next flight by yourself. I can't carry you.'

Dario began hauling himself up the steps using his arms and his one good leg, but it was slow going. Alarmingly, his shot leg was starting to flicker below the knee – appearing less solid than the rest of him, and sometimes fading away almost entirely. The droids would be here before Dario was even halfway up. Raffi puffed his way to Floor Nine. The redhead was gone. He dropped Jonah onto a bed, making him cry out in pain. Sal had already piled up six of the beds near the top of the stairs in preparation for use. Of course none could be launched until Dario had arrived.

⏳

'Dario took a hit in the leg,' Raffi told Sal. 'I'm going to try and buy him some time so he can get up here.' He took up a position on the stairs just below the roof beams of Floor Eight and trained his gunsight on the top of the stairwell leading from Floor Seven. According to the digital readout on his gun, it had nine more rounds. Dario was a pathetic sight, crawling his way up the steps, one at a time. The slow flickering had now spread to the rest of his leg and the fades were slightly lengthier each time. The first two droids appeared at the top of the steps. Raffi aimed carefully before firing, conscious of the need to make each round count. Both droids keeled backwards down the stairs, then disappeared. More droids came, too fast to allow time for precise aiming. He fired four times. Three droids fell back the way they had come. Another kept coming. By the time he was despatched, Raffi had just three rounds left, and Dario was still eight steps from the top. This was going to be very tight.

He ran down to Dario, and began trying to pull him up the steps, making the big lad growl, but not noticeably speeding him up. Three more droids appeared, and Dario still had five more steps to climb. The first droid took aim, but Raffi blasted him into non-existence before he could get off a shot. The second fired his weapon, blowing a hole in the step next to where Raffi was standing. Raffi fired off his last two rounds while manhandling Dario up the last couple of steps with his other hand. Not surprisingly, both his shots missed, but it hardly mattered. They were safely on Floor Nine, and Sal was already lining up the first bed.

Raffi felt at the very end of his energy. He would have given anything to lie down on one of the beds and fall into oblivion, but instead he had to get ready to launch them.

'Let go,' he ordered, once the droids were close enough.

The bed rollercoastered downwards and Raffi watched the robots tumble like skittles before it, but this time he felt no elation. A cheap victory, he reflected, staving off the inevitable defeat. The situation was now worse than hopeless. With Dario and Jonah down and immobile, tactical retreats further up the tower were out of the question. He and Sal would have to fight their last stand here, with just nine more beds.

He looked at Sal as she helped him move the next bed into launching position, but her face was unreadable. She must know they would soon be either captured or killed, but he also knew she would do everything in her power to defy that fate. Meanwhile, below them, more droids clambered over the smoking corpses of their digital dead, straight into the path of another speeding metal cot.

Mira appeared at the top of the steps.

'She won't come down,' she said to Raffi. 'I told her what you said I should tell her, but she won't talk to me and won't move from where she is.'

Sal looked up at the girl, then turned to Raffi. 'What's she going on about?'

'She told me there's a girl up at the top of the tower. I thought it might have been Anna.'

Sal immediately dropped the bed they were holding, causing it to fall on Raffi's foot.

'Owww! What the…?'

He turned, clutching his foot, to see Sal racing up the steps.

'Sal, get down here. I need you. For pity's sake. How'm I going to do this on my own?'

Sal stopped halfway up. 'Come with me, if you like,' she said.

'And leave these two to the robots? Are you crazy?'

'It's hopeless anyway,' said Sal. 'You know that as well as

I do. We've got no more ammo. Just seven more beds. We can't survive this unless we keep climbing.' She looked down at Dario and Jonah, stretched out on mattresses on the bare stone floor. 'And they can't climb.'

'She's right, mate' muttered Dario sleepily. 'Save yourselves.'

'No,' cried Raffi. 'No to the lot of you. I'm staying right here.' Using all his strength he hauled the bed into position. 'Seven beds,' he muttered. 'Should be good for another thirty of 'em. It'll give you two time to get up to the next level if you start now.'

'We're not going anywhere, Raf,' said Jonah. 'I've got a vicious projectile burn in my side. And Dario's temporal field is…' He didn't finish the sentence, but his meaning could be read clearly enough in his bleak expression.

Raffi let go of the bed and watched it crash into another four robots. 'Well then this is where we stand and fight,' he said, tears forming in his eyes. He looked up towards Sal. She was gone – as he knew she would be.

CHAPTER TWENTY-FIVE

⧗

HE USED TO BE A KILLER BUT HE'S ALRIGHT NOW

Barely able to stand now, let alone fight, Raffi started dragging another bed towards the edge of the stairwell. His aching muscles were strained to their limits, yet the bed was barely moving. The clatter of footsteps below was getting louder.

'Save yourself, mate,' came Dario's faint voice. 'You're running out of time.'

'I'll help you if you like.'

Raffi felt a gentle push from the other end of the bed. He roused himself. Mira Chailin was looking at him with her green, wide-spaced eyes.

Together they manoeuvred the bed to the lip of the staircase. They were only just in time. The closest android was eight steps from the top when they let go. He and four of his fellows were swept away.

The girl was slight, but she had energy and enthusiasm which made up somewhat for her lack of upper-body strength. Together they began to move the fifth bed into position.

'Why are you helping us?' Raffi asked her. 'I thought you believed in all this.'

'I sometimes think…,' she said. 'about my life before. I don't know why, but when you asked me if I wanted to go home, it started me thinking that maybe, actually, I do.'

'Well, thanks, Mira. I can't promise that we'll get you home.'

'I know that,' she smiled. 'But it's worth a try isn't it?' They launched the bed and more robots tumbled. 'Why are they trying to kill you?' she asked him. 'You seem like good people.'

'We're not Seed Race,' he told her. 'We only came here to rescue Sal's sister.'

'Shh,' said Mira, putting her finger to her lips. 'Can you hear?'

'Hear what?'

'Exactly.'

Raffi looked at her. Then he understood what she meant. There was no sound coming from the stairwell. Had they killed all the droids? He did a quick calculation. Fifteen beds – 75 androids destroyed at most. There had to be more. Perhaps they'd decided on a change of strategy. He ran to the window. No droids in sight. And no Seed Race. Then, at the bottom of the tower, he saw half a dozen white-uniformed figures, perhaps the Floor-Eighters, gingerly emerging from the doorway. Seeing no one about, they broke into a panicked run. Soon they had disappeared over the brow of the hill.

Raffi turned from the window. He sank into a seated position, leaned back against the wall and closed his eyes. He wanted to let sleep take him, but knew that wasn't an option. After a few moments, he blinked and opened his eyes. Mira was crouched by Dario, who was now asleep, mopping his forehead with a damp towel. He had lost much of his colour, and the flickering had now spread as far as his chest. The fades had lengthened to about five seconds, and he was in danger of becoming indistinguishable from his bedspread. Jonah, by contrast, was looking better. He was sitting up, eyes half open.

'Do you have a medical kit here?' Raffi asked Mira.

'There's one in the bathroom,' she replied, springing into action. She returned with a small black box, which opened to the pressure of her thumb. Raffi glanced at the array of tools, bandages and bottles. He held up one of the bottles and read out the label:

AUTOLYTIC DEBRIDEMENT SOLUTION
Stimulates the body's fluids and enzymes to facilitate the removal of devitalised tissue while preserving viable tissue. Boosts naturally occurring growth factors and cytokines to encourage skin regeneration and wound closure.

He looked at Mira with raised eyebrows. 'Sounds good – for Jonah at least. Why don't you give it a go?'

Raffi was looking at Dario and wondering what medicine could repair a temporal field, when a noise made him turn. Staggering towards him was a badly damaged warrior-droid. One of its arms dangled uselessly – fortunately its gun-carrying one – and it was moving in a jerky, erratic fashion, but closing on him fast. As the droid raised its good arm to strike him, Raffi bashed it on the neck with the handle of his gun. The robot teetered for a moment before crashing to the floor. Raffi had raised his arm ready to smash the thing's face in when he was stopped by a yell from Jonah.

He looked up, still poised to strike.

'We can "turn" it,' croaked Jonah, struggling to sit up.

'Lie back,' ordered Mira. 'And keep still.' She was trying to remove bits of blood-soaked shirt from the wound in Jonah's side.

Raffi looked down at the sparking, fizzing thing at his feet, waiting defiantly for oblivion. 'Can't see the point,' he said.

'Could be useful,' grimaced Jonah. Then he gave a short cry of shock and pain as Mira began dabbing the solution on his raw flesh.

Raffi crouched down to try to locate the droid's control panel. The robot made feeble chopping motions against his elbow, still attempting to follow its preprogrammed instructions to destroy. Raffi pressed the scanpad on the solar plexus, but the abdominal panel refused to open. Michael Storm's was not an authorised thumbprint. He retrieved a pair of pincers from the medical box and used this as a lever to force the panel open. He studied the personality dials. The settings for Aggression, Obedience and Herd Psychology were set to maximum. Being a fighter-droid, there were no dials for traits like Proactiveness, Agreeableness or Empathy as one might expect to find on a service machine. Raffi moved the settings to their midpoints, and the droid stopped its chopping.

'What now, Jonah?'

'You should see a keypad below the personality dials. Key in the following number: seven-oh-six-one-five-two. It's a generic Secrocon passcode I learned while I was in the PEC.'

'It works,' said Raffi as a screen embedded in the droid's chest flicked on.

'Okay, now choose "system preferences" from the menu bar. Raffi touched the appropriate area of the screen, and options stacked up holographically above it.

'Choose "tasks". You should see our names and identities coming up, along with instructions to kill us.'

Miniature holograms of himself, Dario, Jonah and Sal, together with their bio-data codes, materialised in the air before him. The word 'exterminate' appeared beneath each figure. Raffi noted that his and Dario's faces were blank, thanks to the CID masks they were still wearing, but the biodata would have been enough for the droids to identify them.

'Highlight "exterminate",' said Jonah, 'and replace with "assist".' Raffi did so, then closed the abdominal panel. He looked into the black holes that counted for eyes.

'What's your name, droid?'

A crackle and hiss came through the mouth slit. 'My-name-is-S-T-A-N-that-is-Security-Troop-Appliance-Number-one-five-seven-four-nine-eight-two-six-double-oh-four.' The voice was a monotonous drone, with equalised spacing between words and scarcely any intonation, making it difficult to catch sense. Communications were not a major priority for these specialised killing machines.

'That's quite a mouthful,' said Raffi. 'Mind if we just call you STAN?'

'Negative---all-Secrocon-warrior-droids-have-the-S-T-A-N-prefix---it-would-not-be-an-appropriate-appellation.'

'Too bad, STAN,' said Raffi, getting back to his feet. 'That's your name. Now, can you fix yourself?'

The robot rose to a sitting position causing the broken panel door in its stomach to swing open. 'Partial-battlefield-repair-may-be-possible---status-report---damage-to-right-triaxial-shoulder-joint-affecting-movement-of-right-arm---damage-to-left-thigh-bi-articular-muscle-affecting-motor-stability----damage-to-power-supply-to-omni-direction-cam-in-left-eye-and-three-degree-freedom-in-neck-due-to-recent-impact-with-base-of-your-gun---damage-to-'

'Okay, okay,' said Raffi. 'I get the message. You're not a well boy. Well, listen STAN, see what you can do about fixing yourself up, and then maybe you can go and give Mira a hand over there.'

Raffi went over to Dario, who had awoken and was muttering to himself deliriously. 'How you doing?'

'Huh? Who's that?' He was sweating.

'It's me.'

'Uh. Raffi. Can you get me some water, mate?'

Raffi went to get water from the bathroom. He glanced out of the window. All still quiet. Too quiet. The landscape was completely devoid of life. Drak's droid army were up to something. He just wished he knew what.

He gave the water to Dario, who drank it down in one gulp. 'Thanks for staying,' he said, handing back the cup. 'Appreciate it.'

'Hey, what did you expect? I know you'd have done the same for me.' It was hard conversing with someone who was visible for less than five out of every ten seconds.

What's up with the droids? Have we killed 'em all?'

'I don't know. It's all quiet at the moment.'

'Listen mate. I realise I haven't got long. I can hardly remember my leg now, let alone feel it. And the rest of me is starting to go the same way.'

'You'll be fine, Dario. Nine lives. Remember?'

'Not this time, mate. Let's be honest with ourselves. Listen, if you get the chance, tell Sal I… understand she did what she had to do for her sister, and I still… I still love her.'

'You'll tell her that yourself, my friend.' He clutched his hand as it faded, then weakly reappeared. 'By the way, we've got a new nurse on the ward. His name is STAN, and he used to be a killer, but he's much nicer now. He'll be with you shortly.'

Dario looked up at the droid, who was busy welding the wound on its neck, and groaned.

STAN limped over to Jonah and took a look at what Mira was doing. 'I-have-been-programmed-in-human-battlefield-injury-surgical-procedures,' he intoned. 'Did-you-administer-antibiotic-prophylaxis-before-applying-autolytic-debridement-solution?'

Mira looked at him, her lower lip quivering. 'N-no. I didn't.' She quietly slid aside to let STAN take over.

'Hey, STAN,' said Raffi, indicating Dario. 'This one's more urgent. Can you deal with him first.'

STAN briefly assessed the fading boy. 'Direct-hit-in-lower-leg-from-Temp-Fi-Er-Six-laser-projectile---temporal-field-damage-has-spread-to-eighty-percent-of-victim's-body--total-field-erasure-will-occur-in-less-than-three-minutes.'

'Can you save him?'

'Amputation-is-the-one-remaining-hope.'

'You mean you'll have to amputate his leg?'

'Yes.'

'Ah, mate!' cried Dario. 'Not me leg!'

'Do it!' said Raffi. 'Do it now, while there's still time.'

STAN pointed at Dario's head and a brief spark emerged from his fingertip. Dario fell asleep. STAN then unscrewed his other hand and, from a door in his thigh, he extracted a gun-type prosthesis, which he fitted to his wrist.

'Pull-up-his-trouser-leg.'

Raffi did so, then stood back as a stream of orange laser light poured out of STAN's gun hand, slicing through Dario's leg in a gentle curve just below his knee.

'Remove-the-severed-part.'

Raffi swallowed and then picked up Dario's lower leg, which was now flickering much more frequently. It came away easily. In the brief seconds of its visibility, he glimpsed at the top end, white bone and bloody tissue. He placed it at the end of the bed while STAN got on with repairing the stump. The cut had left flaps of skin dangling beneath the wound site. STAN exchanged his gun hand for another, smaller implement and applied this to the skin flaps, closing them together over the wound to make a smooth, rounded stump. Raffi, watching this, scarcely noticed that the severed part of the leg had now disappeared from the end of the bed.

In the medical case STAN found a packet of chrono-domes – miniature chronospheres that could speed up time, and therefore the healing process – and applied one of these to the stump. 'Within-an-hour-the-wound-will-be-fully-healed,' he predicted.

Fifteen more minutes went by. Raffi watched from the steps as STAN supervised Mira in the dressing of Jonah's wound using fast-acting nanocrystalline silver beneath the bandages. Strangely, as he viewed the missing part of Dario, he was finding it harder to remember that he'd ever had a leg there. Even knowing that this was the effect of temporal field erasure didn't help: the new, reduced Dario was fast becoming the only Dario there had ever been. And, as he watched, the new, reduced Dario was becoming more solid before his eyes, as his damaged temporal field gradually rebuilt itself.

With Jonah and Dario now both sleeping soundly, Raffi decided it would be a good time to go and check up on Sal. As he began mounting the steps, he heard a massive rumbling explosion far below and the whole building shook, causing him to lose his footing and tumble to the floor.

He groaned, clutching his elbow and hip. 'What in hooly was that?'

Mira ran to the window. 'Oh dear!' she said. 'Raffi, you'd better come and look.'

He joined her at the window. A single droid was standing on the hillside facing them at a distance of about 50 metres. He was aiming a shoulder-launched energy projectile cannon in their direction. There was smoke at the base of the tower, and as it cleared they saw a large hole had been blasted in its side. A second pulse of laser-energy burst from the muzzle of the cannon and exploded against the building, causing Mira to fall on top of Raffi as they were both knocked violently to the floor.

'I'm sorry,' she murmured, hurriedly getting back to her feet.

The floor was no longer even. The whole tower was visibly listing in the direction of the hillside.

'They're going to knock the tower down,' said Raffi. 'Listen, Mira. Thanks for all you've done. But you should get out of here while you still can.'

'They'll kill me for sure,' she said. 'They see me as one of you now.'

'No,' said Raffi. 'You just tell them we've been keeping you prisoner.'

'It's no good, Raffi.' Her green eyes looked excited, almost feverish. 'You told me I was going home today. Well, what hope is there of that if I leave now? While I'm with you, there's still a chance.'

There was another explosion, and they were thrown again to the floor. The floor was sloping at almost 10 degrees. The mattresses and beds were starting to slide towards them. STAN was clinging on to the bannister rail. 'I'm scared,' Mira whispered.

'Me too,' said Raffi. He wondered how many more such blasts the building could take.

CHAPTER TWENTY-SIX

THE LEVITATOR RIDE

'Get up! Get up!' Sal shouted.

Raffi opened his eyes. She was standing at the top of the stairs, smiling like she'd just seen some kind of holy vision.

'Come up here now!' she yelled.

'The whole building's about to fall,' Raffi pointed out. 'What the hooly difference will it make to go up another flight?'

'All the difference,' beamed Sal. 'We're going to escape. I managed to summon a levitator from the top floor. It'll take us right out of here to whatever's above us.'

Raffi got to his feet and pulled Mira with him.

'Sal, you'll have to give us a hand with Jonah and Dario.'

Sal hesitated, then started running down the steps.

STAN had already picked up Dario and slung him over his shoulder with effortless ease.

'It's okay,' said Raffi, seeing Sal's shocked look. 'STAN's been "turned". He's on our side now.'

He and Sal picked up Jonah and then promptly dropped

him again as another blast hit the building and they were thrown to the floor.

There came a terrible groaning sound from all around them, and the whole room listed to an angle approaching 15 degrees. Cracks began to race through the white walls in all directions, wide enough to show clear daylight through them.

'This is it!' cried Raffi. 'We're going to fall!'

The beams in the ceiling began to crack and splinter, and a roughly circular area on the far side, just near the stairwell, was punched out of it and fell with a deafening crash to the floor, just a few metres from where they were lying. This was followed by a dirty, transparent column about four metres in diameter, that slid rapidly through the hole and fell heavily to the ground, sending up clouds of choking dust. The column glowed through its powdery exterior with an inner yellow light.

'The levitator!' cried Sal with a look of horror. 'The upper floor must have given way beneath it. I left Anna in there!' She seemed almost scared to approach it, fearing what she might find. Shaking, she pressed her palm to a panel on the transparent surface. It pulsed pink, and a section of the column slid upwards. A female figure lay curled on the light disc floor. Sal rushed in and took her sister in her arms, obscuring her from Raffi's sight, but he saw enough to know she was okay. Raffi and Mira dragged Jonah while STAN conveyed Dario through the levitator doorway and onto the yellow light disc. Once they were in, Sal released Anna and pressed a button in a metallic panel. The light disc began to rise swiftly through the column, carrying them with it. The girl leaned weakly against the levitator wall. Raffi recognised her immediately. She looked younger, yet somehow older than the girl he remembered. A pale sallowness had replaced the bloom in her cheeks, and a lost and bewildered look had supplanted the bright intelligence of her eyes, yet it was most definitely her: not the ridiculous fantasy creature cooked up by him and Brigitte, but the original Anna Morrow. Her subtle beauty – infinitely superior to that of her crudely fashioned doppelganger – was painful to witness now that it bore the mark of a confused and traumatised mind. Guilt pierced him like an arrow.

He quickly turned away and focused instead on the view through the dusty walls of the column, trying to make sense of the chaotic scene outside. When Sal had summoned the levitator, its enclosing column, designed to drop through the hollow centre of the tower's conical red steeple and upper floors, had instead encountered a damaged edifice, leaning several degrees off the vertical. So the column must have missed its slot and smashed through the roof of the building, coming to rest on Floor Nine. Now, as they ascended, the structural fabric of the toppling tower appeared to be ripping itself apart on the glass-like finger that enclosed them. Within seconds they were clear of it and racing up towards the blue imitation sky. Beneath the light disc floor, Raffi glimpsed the white tower, with its blackened wounds, begin its final, groaning descent to the undulating green carpet a hundred metres below. The steeple, with a huge rent through its middle, seemed to drop through the shoulders of the tower, tipping forwards until it fell free in a long, graceful dive to the verdant slopes, where it lay like the broken beak of a giant prehistoric bird. The tower itself seemed to fall apart even before it landed, breaking into huge fragments of rounded, chalk-white wall, like pieces of a shattered coconut, which sent up explosions of grey dust as they landed. Did the armed units witness their escape, or did they think they had perished with the tower? Raffi had no idea, nor time to speculate, as they closed in on their new destination.

Above them, the sky was now close enough to be revealed as a concave, blue-painted surface. The levitator slowed as they passed out of the vast brightness of the Garden and into a small, utilitarian room, far more typical of the claustrophobic Underside of the Sphere. The door slid upwards and Sal helped Anna out of the levitator. Raffi, Mira and STAN followed, bearing their injured companions.

'Anna,' said Raffi, holding out his hand to the girl. She looked at him, but said and did nothing. Her face showed no sign of recognition.

He turned to Sal. 'Has she said anything to you?'

Sal shook her head and tenderly wiped a strand of hair from her sister's eye. 'What do we do now?' asked Mira.

Raffi had no time to answer. The wall in front of them softened and rippled into something with the texture of fabric, then parted like a curtain. They now saw that they were at one end of a long, wide corridor. Between them and the rest of the corridor stood Chrono-Sensei Avon Drak, flanked by half a dozen armed and green-uniformed guards.

Anna, on seeing Avon, began to wail like a scared animal. She tried to break free of Sal's embrace.

Drak was his usual distinguished self, but the smile and some of the calm self-assurance was gone, and the handsome grey eyes now quivered like a pair of angry moths. 'We brought down the tower,' he snarled, 'knowing that the only way out of there was to come up here. You fell very neatly into our trap. Now get over there, all of you.' He gestured towards an alcove at the back of the room. STAN, still programmed to 'assist' Dario, Raffi and Sal, moved instead towards Drak, his gun hand taking aim as he approached. Before he had managed three paces, he was caught in a crossfire from three of the guards, and the droid was no more than a wisp of smoke in the air. Dario, still unconscious, fell heavily to the floor.

'Move!' yelled Drak to the others. Raffi dragged Dario into the alcove and propped him up against the wall. Soon they were all there, facing the muzzles of six guns. Anna continued to moan, despite Sal's attempts to comfort her. Mira looked up at Raffi and smiled sadly. He felt her grasp his hand.

'I'm sorry,' he whispered to her.

'Don't be,' she said. 'I have no regrets.'

'Be brave,' he mumbled, unsure if he was saying it to her or himself.

'Take aim!' said Drak.

CHAPTER TWENTY-SEVEN

⏳

THE BROKEN DARKNESS GENERATOR

There was a metallic hum as the automatic sound sensors of each gun locked onto the heartbeat of its target. Fingers embraced the triggers. Raffi wished he could feel a sense of resolution, of calm. His heart only raced with dumb, animal dread. But then, instead of pulverising fire and death, there came a clear, high voice, yelling 'Stop!'

The familiar voice came from further up the corridor, beyond the line of marksmen. In unison, they turned. Raffi strained to see over their shoulders, unable to believe he was still alive. He glimpsed the Chronomaster's black cube hastening towards them, accompanied by around twenty blue-uniformed loyalists.

Seeing themselves outnumbered, or perhaps because of an instinctive respect for the Chronomaster, Drak's green-uniformed guards immediately downed their weapons and moved to one or other side of the corridor to allow the cube to pass between them. Avon Drak wore the look of a man thwarted, though the smile that quickly resurfaced on his lips did not suggest one necessarily beaten.

'Chronomaster Carinae,' said Drak, bowing towards the dark shape. 'What a pleasure to see you down here. To what do we owe the pleasure?'

Carinae's lilting voice emerged from the blackness. 'Why were you about to kill these people, Avon? I believe that some of them, at least, were among the group of Seed Race Elect I spoke to this morning.'

Avon's smile broadened. 'Chronomaster, these are imposters – a bunch of escaped Re-Ed inmates, along with their cronies and accomplices. They destroyed upwards of 40 droids today, and killed at least one human officer. They're not suitable material for the Garden.'

'On the contrary, Avon. The resourcefulness they've shown in escaping your clutches today would seem to make them ideal Seed Race material. You, on the other hand, have proved deceitful.'

'I, Chronomaster? Deceitful?'

'I have learned a few things today, Avon. A girl called Lastara Blue came to me earlier and told me about some of your activities. She didn't mean to betray you – she really did believe that all your actions were undertaken on my authority. It came as quite a shock to her to realise that these activities of yours – sabotaging the Topside and carrying out cruel experiments on teenagers, to name but two – were done entirely without my knowledge. Do you believe you run this place, Chrono-Sensei, is that it?'

Avon shrugged and smiled. 'It's not a question of believing, Edo. I know it for a fact.' As he said this, he grabbed a gun from the hand of a nearby guard and took a wild swing at the top half of the cube, his arms and upper body momentarily disappearing as they were engulfed by the inky blackness. There was a sound like the violent breaking of glass, and the dark cube disappeared. Edo Carinae sat revealed, blinking in the sudden, unexpected rush of light. As

Raffi stared at the long-hidden features now revealed, he recalled the shock of Slim Trifid and Puppis Nova when they first glimpsed Carinae's time-disfigured face. Their gasp of horror could not have been dissimilar to the instinctive murmur of revulsion that echoed around the room now.

The face was unbearable. If it had been simply alien or reptillian, Raffi would have coped better. What made it worse, much worse, was the fact that it was almost human. Here and there were haunting reminders of the original man. Trapped within deep craters of scarred, scaly, greenish-brown skin, to either side of a cruelly thin beak of a nose, was a pair of watchful, brown – human – eyes. And between the twisted pout of his grey lips and a set of misaligned teeth gleamed a smooth, pink, healthy tongue. Edo was sprawled in a hover-chair, his withered body warped, so that his hip rested on the seat and his feet, dangling from thin, useless legs, faced to the side. Extending upwards from the back of the chair was a metal pole supporting a thick square of blue translucent material like a small roof. The square was chipped on one side and spidered with cracks. This was the object that Drak had broken.

Much too late, the Chronomaster raised a pair of deformed, skeletal hands to cover his face. 'You have broken my darkness generator, my photon blocker.' He spoke shakily, evidently in extreme distress. 'Why, Avon?'

'To show people what you are.' Drak turned to the dumbfounded blue uniforms. 'Is this really a man you wish to follow?' he asked them. 'Scarcely a man at all, is he? Now take him, and his chair, to Holding Room One.'

The men hesitated. Raffi could see the desperate confusion on their faces. In those still, tense seconds, a fireball of hysterical energy suddenly erupted from the alcove near where Raffi stood and crashed into Avon, knocking the gun from his hand. Anna Morrow! Avon swiftly recovered his balance and knocked her spinning sideways into a wall. This casual action jolted Raffi almost as though he'd been struck himself. Before Avon could regain his gun, Raffi ran up and kicked it away, before trying to push the chrono-sensei back against the wall. Avon was strong, and Raffi quickly found himself in a desperate tussle with him. 'Kill this man!' Avon yelled at his men, but Carinae, no longer bothering to hide his face, immediately countermanded the order. 'Don't shoot.'

Raffi managed to get Avon into a necklock, squashing his throat and preventing him from saying any more.

At last, the blue-uniformed officers seemed to make up their minds. They trained their guns on the chrono-sensei.

'Thankyou, Raffi,' said Carinae. 'Now please move away from him.'

Raffi went back to the alcove where Sal was tending to Anna. He noticed Mira looking admiringly at him.

When he looked back, Raffi saw that Carinae now cradled a weapon of his own: it had the same pinecone-shaped muzzle of a temp fi-er, but this one was larger, and golden in colour.

Drak drew back at the sight of it, his eyes, for the first time, showing fear.

'I found this in your notorious Punishment and Experimentation Centre, Avon. I've been studying it today, and it is a most curious weapon. It could, of course, obliterate you in time and space. But somehow I don't think that would be the right kind of punishment, do you? After all, it's important for all our sakes that we remember Avon Drak, if only to ensure that we never make the same mistake again of trusting someone like you. But this gun has another capacity. It can send its victims into Zeno Space, that strange dimension where everything is just a little bit further than one expects, and always just out of reach. In Zeno Space, so I've read, space and time are infinitely divisible and a moving object must pass through eternity simply to get from A to B. As the victim begins to move back across the few centimetres that separate his world from ours, he soon understands how unbridgeable those few centimetres are. Like Tantalus, he can see the object of his desire, he can almost touch it, but he can never reach it. But you know all about that, don't you, Avon, having despatched numerous teenagers there for up to a week at a time, or so I've been told. But for your crimes – and I am only now becoming aware of the full extent of them – a week doesn't seem quite enough. I think a longer sentence would be appropriate. How about… eternity?'

'Listen,' said Avon. 'You need me. You're getting on now, Edo. I virtually run the Chronosphere these days as you well know. I manage Secrocon and recruit for the Seed Race. You have the vision, but you don't have the energy any more. You need me. We're partners, Edo. We've been partners for a long time. We shouldn't just throw it all away over a simple misunderstanding.'

'Misunderstanding!' Carinae's rubbery grey lips twisted into a snarl. Tiny nostrils flared at the base of his thin hook of a nose. He twisted his head round so that it was half buried in the upholstered back of his chair. Moisture welled on his cracked cheek, just below his eye. 'I had hoped for something better from you, Avon. An apology at least.'

'Let me explain something to you –' began Drak.

'Silence!' yelled Carinae. He abruptly uncoiled himself and levelled the gun at the chrono-sensei. 'I've heard enough, too much… May Bo forgive me,' he murmured.

'No,' screamed Avon. 'No!'

Carinae swallowed, shut his eyes. Raffi didn't see him pull the trigger, but a cone of pale pink light suddenly blew outwards from the muzzle and enclosed Drak. Still visible within the cone, he punched and kicked at the walls of light that surrounded him in a desperate attempt to escape. His efforts made no impact. Gradually the cone shrank to a narrow pink beam, which disappeared as Carinae released the trigger.

In the silence that followed, Raffi stared at the empty space that had once contained Avon Drak. He tried to picture him now, just centimetres away from where he'd been, embarking on the long and fruitless journey back, racing, sprinting, rampaging through infinitessimal fractions of a millimetre and never making any actual progress. The thought stunned him, as it seemed to everyone else. It was Edo who finally broke the silence. 'Could someone please turn down these bright lights. I find them most uncomfortable.'

One of the officers obediently dimmed the overheads in the corridor, and Raffi was not actually sorry to see Edo's hideous features fall back into their accustomed obscurity.

'You will forgive me,' said Carinae, 'if I do not seem myself just now. The scale of Avon's treachery, and the suffering he has caused in my name, are hard to absorb all at once. I wish to offer my thanks, however, to you brave and resourceful young people for confronting him and for your help in overcoming him. I will never be able to forgive myself for my blindness in trusting him. But there we are. Perhaps Avon was right about one thing: maybe I am getting too old for this game.

'Now, before anything else, we must reestablish normal conditions Topside.' He turned to one of the blue-uniformed officers. 'Chief Sentinel Aston Brigg, please give orders to restore the temp-al chambers and cooling systems to working order, and send up a medical team to take care of the sick and wounded. Also send a team of engineers and technicians to take stock of infrastructure damage.'

Raffi yawned. He was scarcely able to keep his eyes open. Seven hours ago he'd been battling Potter Logan's forces on the back of Milla's hoverbike. It had been non-stop ever since. Now all he wanted was a little food, and then some rest.

CHAPTER TWENTY-EIGHT

⏳

THE SCALE OF THE CATASTROPHE

A guard directed Raffi to a room off another corridor a few floors up from the Garden Levitator Terminus. The room contained an armchair and a sofa. A muted sensovision flickered in the corner like a cosy fireplace, beaming comfortingly familiar images of old shows. He had even been allocated a MAID by the name of Suzy – all 'on the house', courtesy of the Chronomaster. Suzy served him an invitroburger on tomato-bread with sea kale and a glass of warm pecan milk. Raffi soon fell asleep in front of the sensovision. The following morning, he received a visit from Dario, who glided in on a hoverchair. Raffi had a vague recollection that Dario used to have two fully functioning legs and had even been something of a star athlete in his day, but he thought it might have been a dream.

Dario laughed when he told him this. 'Mate, you've got an imagination! But, speaking of the old stump, I do have a hankering for something a little easier on the eye and more functional maybe. As soon as we get out of here, I'll look into it. You never know, maybe they can fix it so I end up as a champion jock, just like in your dream!'

They met Sal in a canteen on Level 142 – fourteen stories up – for breakfast. She looked tired. 'Anna's still not saying anything,' she said. 'The HUTT scan showed signs of altered brain activity, which they say is consistent with post-traumatic stress disorder.'

'Does she know who you are?' asked Raffi.

'I can't be sure. She senses I mean well. She seems very interested in me and what I have to say, but I can't say how much she understands. When we get home I'll take her to some old haunts of ours and show her some home holoflicks. Maybe, in time, she'll start to come out of that horrid place she's now inhabiting.'

'I hope so,' said Raffi. His infatuation with Anna now seemed a foolish, trivial thing. Maybe one day, years from now, he and she could meet again in better circumstances and, just maybe, the spark they had both felt during that brief encounter seven months earlier could be rekindled. For such a day, he could live in hope.

'I must get back to her now,' said Sal, 'but before I do, I want to apologise to both of you.' A look of contrition dawned hesitantly on her hard little face. With her blue hair, big eyes and pursed lips, she looked like a naughty pixie. 'My behaviour yesterday was pretty appalling, and you two bore the brunt of it. I want to know if we're still friends.'

'Of course,' grinned Dario, and he leaned over the table to smother her in a bear hug. She emerged from this to look at Raffi.

Raffi did his best to look forgiving as he smiled and shook her hand. But deep down he remained troubled by something

Sal had done yesterday – something unforgivable, while they were in Secrocon HQ.

As if reading his thoughts, Sal said: 'While we were in Sphere 12, I believe I may even have killed a man called…' She fumbled for a note she'd written to herself. '…Cy Vesta. I'm going to find out who his family is and I'm going to compensate them in any way I can.'

Raffi had no memory of this man or of Sal killing him – and from Dario's blank look it appeared that he didn't either. But it did seem, to Raffi at least, as though something very serious like a murder had taken place, because it had left him with a sense that however normal and friendly Sal was now, and however much she remained a part of their gang in the future, he would never be able to feel quite the same towards her again.

After Sal had left them, Jonah appeared with Lastara. Jonah had fully recovered from his injury, thanks to the nanocrystalline silver and several hours of chrono-dome treatment, and he walked unaided to the table. He looked ecstatically happy. Lastara had dispensed with the regal attire in favour of one of her usual pastel-coloured metallic outfits. Her customary healthy glow had been replaced by a wan and troubled look. She avoided all talk about recent events and the role she'd played in them. The name Avon Drak didn't cross her lips. Instead, she talked quietly about her plans for the future. She seemed to believe that the Topside would be rebuilt and that life would simply resume there as before. Jonah was only too happy to indulge her in this fantasy.

After breakfast, Raffi heard a different version of events from Suzy. 'Engineers and medics,' she informed him, 'have made their initial report on the Topside. Avon Drak's actions have caused widespread devastation. Between them, the gang violence, dysentery, hyperthermia and starvation killed over a thousand Topsiders and left more than three thousand with injuries, which are currently being treated in the Secrocon Med Centre. Scarcely a building remains intact and over half have been reduced to rubble. As Drak could not have acted alone, the Chronomaster has ordered a thorough internal investigation to root out any co-conspirators. Because of the scale of the catastrophe, Time Store Incorporated will, we are sure, have to submit to an external investigation by Londaris Criminal Justice Department. In anticipation of this requirement, we are currently in the process of accelerating the time velocity of the Chronosphere to bring it into temporal alignment with the outside world. Estimated Time of Alignment is twenty-five weeks. It is highly probable, Raffi, that you and your friends will be required to attend the investigation, but we understand that you won't wish to be detained here for the next six months or longer. For this reason, we give you leave to depart as soon as you like. Your identities are all logged into our database, so we will have no trouble contacting you when the time comes. Remember to pick up your hyperdilatory chrono-capsule as you leave.'

'My what?' asked Raffi.

'Your hyperdilatory chrono-capsule. It's a Moon Effect preventative.'

'The Moon Effect! So it *is* real, then!'

'Yes, it's a side effect of living at these superfast speeds. Your physical form has taken up less space than the time it has consumed, causing a small imbalance within you. When you leave here, you may find your body begins to age a little more quickly. It's barely noticeable for someone who's been in here for just nine months, as you have. Nevertheless, it's worth spending a little time in hyperdilation just to be safe.'

'And what happens in hyperdilation?'

'For a brief period, your physical form takes up *more* space than the time it consumes.'

'And what does that mean in words I can understand?'

'You disappear briefly – not in space, but in time. From your point of view, you will enter the capsule in the evening, when you normally go to bed, and then – in what seems like no time at all – you'll wake up and it will be morning.'

'And what happens to people who've been here a long time?' Raffi was thinking of Jonah and Lastara.

'They will have to do a lot more hypercap time. The Chronomaster himself is the longest-living resident of the Chronosphere. He was already 80 when he entered the Sphere and he has now lived a total of 200 years in subjective terms. He has decided, for personal reasons, not to do any hypercap time. After a long and often difficult life, he says that the prospect of death is very comforting. When the Chronosphere begins to approach normal time, he will start to age very rapidly. By the time it docks, he will be long dead. In the months remaining to him, he will create a holographic replicon of himself into which he will pour as many of his own thoughts and memories as he can. He hopes the replicon will serve as an adequate surrogate for the purposes of interrogation by the investigating authorities.'

When Suzy had finished her report, Raffi called Jonah. 'What are you going to do?' he asked him.

'About what?'

'This Moon Effect thing. It's not good news for you and Lastara, is it?'

'It was always going to happen,' said Jonah. 'I just preferred not to worry about it.'

'You could do a stint in this hypercap thingy. That should sort you both out.'

There was a pause. 'Yeah. That should sort us out.'

🕑

An hour later, Suzy informed Raffi that the first of the tempal chambers – number seven, which lay at the end of Interim Avenue – had been restored to working order, and he was free to leave. To get there, he would have to re-enter the Topside on the western side of Tomorrow Fields near a copse by a stream, then make a short journey on foot to the perimeter. He would need to wear a coolsuit, as the Topside coolers had not yet been repaired. The suit appeared on a hanger next to his bed. It was white and red and made of a shiny, unfamiliar material. It felt chill and moist to the touch, but when Raffi removed his fingers, they were dry. When he put it on, the pleasant coolness reminded him a little of a vapour shower. The facial area was of the same material as the rest of the suit, but translucent. A small plastic filter, which fitted over the mouth and nose, would cool the air sufficiently for breathing Topside. It also gave it a pleasing lemon scent.

As he walked along the corridor towards the levitators, Raffi couldn't help noticing the tension in the faces of the Secrocon personnel that he passed. There was a reckoning to come for the Topside catastrophe, and some of them were going to be exposed as Drakites. Of course, the guilty wouldn't sit mildly for the next six months until the investigators arrived. At some point they would attempt to wrest control of the timeship Chronosphere and decelerate it back out of reach of those who would call them to account, back into the sanctuary of the near-eternal present. And this was a prospect that must keep Edo Carinae awake at night. The mutiny had to come, he just didn't know when.

But this wasn't Raffi's problem. He was leaving, thank Bo. He called his friends and they agreed to meet by the bank of levitators on Level 156. Dario and Sal were both as keen to leave as he was. Jonah and Lastara wouldn't be leaving just yet, but they wanted to come along as far as the temp-al lobby to see the others off.

When they arrived, he saw they were all togged up like him in shiny, stretchy coolsuits. Anna was a quiet, shadowy presence, never straying far from Sal's side. Jonah told Raffi he had booked himself and Lastara in for a programme of hypercap sessions. 'The docs told me it should last about four weeks, then we'll be ready to leave. That'll be just a few seconds of your time, so you won't even have time to miss us.'

They boarded the light disc and it sped them to the surface. Raffi felt no discomfort until the disc stopped and the door slid upwards. It was only momentary, though. The thermostatic fabric of the coolsuit swiftly adapted to the searing heat, and the photosensitive mask simultaneously dimmed in the blinding exterior light, but the suit could do nothing to reduce the harshness of the view that greeted them. The copse by a stream had become a few stalks of brittle, white deadwood next to a bed of parched and cracked yellow earth. They stepped off the light disc and out of the levitator terminus, a dome-topped transparent column that protruded some three metres above the ground. Tomorrow Fields was a wasteland. In every direction, the same arid, bleached and lifeless view assaulted them. This had once been one of the prettiest parts of the Sphere, its lush meadows, shady trees and whispering stream a popular destination for picnic-goers. Raffi had been here many times himself, but now he failed to recognise it.

'This way,' came Jonah's rasping, filtered voice. The others followed as Jonah struck out to the north-west along a faint indentation that had once been a grassy path leading to the exit on Interim Avenue. The air was laden with clouds of orange dust: a mix of dry earth and the ash of hundreds of fires, pumped upwards on the air currents that continued to circulate around the Sphere. The air coming through their heat filters was, though on the warm side, mercifully free of dust. Behind them, through the amber haze, Raffi took a final look at Time Tower, dark and sinuous like a quiescent tornado.

Within ten minutes, they had reached the cool cathedral-like sanctuary of the temp-al lobby. They walked the vast, flat tundra of marble flooring to the temp-al chamber entrance. As they walked, Raffi thought, not for the first time, about the sheer abundance of space in the Chronosphere, and he wondered again how it wasn't visible as an enormous dome from all over Central Londaris.

Lastara gave Dario, Raffi and Sal a hug. 'This is really a farewell for me, not for you,' she said. 'You won't even have time to think of us, I realise that. But spare me a speed-of-light thought at least for the horrors that await me in that beastly hyperwhotsit capsule.'

Raffi was glad to see she wasn't stoned. He didn't dare hope she might have turned some corner. Yet it certainly seemed as though Jonah was having a positive effect on her. 'You'll be fine, Lastara,' he said, kissing her cheek. 'And when it's all over, just think: you'll be able to rejoin the real world.'

'What a squalid thought,' she cried. 'The real world. How perfectly horrid.' She turned to Jonah. 'Remind me, dearie. Why are we doing this?'

'We have no choice my darling,' said Jonah. 'The Chronosphere will be docking shortly anyway. The party's over.'

She turned back to Raffi, then switched her gaze to Dario. 'Oh yes,' she said huskily. 'And what a party it's been.'

'Excuse me, ladies and gentlemen.' It was a grey-suited attendant. 'The temp-al chamber is now ready for boarding.'

Lastara and Jonah gave final hugs and kisses to their

friends and the attendant waved his hand over a panel. Raffi waited for the door to open. Instead he heard a deafening bang and the door blew violently out towards them, its thick steel warping like a billowing curtain. Huge cracks simultaneously spidered their way up the white walls that surrounded the door. Through the opening poured an elongated bubble that quickly expanded to fill the airspace of the lobby. The bubble verged on transparent, although its skin was liquid-shiny and in constant motion, reminding Raffi of the strange coating he'd seen on everything while he'd been desynchronised. And he knew then that he was seeing, once again, that other-worldly interface between two versions of time.

Raffi was now on his back, knocked there by the blast. He was helpless as the bubble pushed on over his body, surrounding, then engulfing him. A terrifying pain seared him, as if every last molecule was being simultaneously shaken, squeezed, repositioned, reconfigured. The stresses, the strains, the heat, the chill, of all his 300 days and nights in the Sphere, rained simultaneously like fire, like hail, on each cell, each nerve. He was a tight roll of twine unravelling, at a speed uncontrollable, a toy boat in a tsunami, borne on forces unimaginable. The grating in his ears was like a giant icecrushing machine. He was sure he was dying.

And then, gradually, the pain began to ease. The fire became hot smoke. The hail became sleet. The ice crusher, distant thunder. He lay there, too weak to move, almost too scared to try, in case he couldn't; feeling older, frailer, in every limb, bone and organ. He groaned. So that was what the Moon Effect felt like.

CHAPTER TWENTY-NINE

⌛

Unmistakable Gleamings of Home

The Chronosphere was a bubble of compressed time. That was how Luther Prefix had described it to Raffi. And the bubble, like all bubbles, had to be kept sealed from the outside world, or else it would, well, burst. 'So,' Raffi thought to himself, as he began groggily to push himself into a seated position, 'what we appear to be facing here is a burst bubble... Something must have gone wrong with the temp-al chamber as the man was opening it, and external time, which moved over half a million times faster than Chronospheric time, had invaded. So instead of a nice gentle reintroduction to normal timespeed, we got the full force of it in a sudden rush. And worse, we got the Moon Effect: payback all in one go, instead of in nice, easy installments.'

One of the almost unfairly wonderful things about the Chronosphere was that it allowed you to live at decelerated time, while your body continued to age at normal time. In other words, so long as you remained in here, your body would age over half a million times more slowly than your lifespeed. The drawback was that once you reentered the outside world, you would have to start paying back the time you had taken, by doing hypercap time. You would step out of the hypercap quite literally an older person. But Raffi wouldn't need hypercap treatment now. He'd become nine months older – all at once. And he felt every single day of it weighing down on him. A tickly sensation near his ears made him touch his face. His fingers encountered a great shrubby mass of hair. A beard! And just look at the state of his nails!

Gradually, as his consciousness began to spread further afield, he noticed he was leaning against a wall. He looked up and was surprised to see the ceiling was no more than two metres above his nose. He also became aware of something uncomfortable digging into his bottom. He moved to see what it was. It looked like a tiny fountain, no bigger than a five u-doll coin, and next to it were two little benches, each one the size of a fingernail clipping. They were like miniature versions of the fountain and benches he had passed not five minutes ago as they were crossing the lobby. Looking again at the familiar shiny pink floor, it suddenly hit him: he was still in the lobby! Only the lobby had shrunk – or else he had become a giant.

A grunting sound to his right nudged Raffi out of his shock. Was that one-legged bushy-bearded fellow next to him Dario? He was exercising his neck muscles and groping his upper arms with yellow-nailed fingers as if not certain they were still his. But above the thick, straggly beard, Raffi recognised his friend's pale blue eyes. There were a few greys in the great brown foliage of his hair and beard, but the voice that now emerged could belong to no other: 'What the hell was that?' Dario murmured. 'It wasn't… Was it?'

'I think it was,' said Raffi. 'And it's turned us into giants… which I hadn't expected.' He glanced around him. It was the lobby alright, now a very modest-scaled room of no more than four metres to a side. The bubble was gone. Or, more accurately, they were all inside the bubble now. Nearby were Sal and Anna, still out cold from the blast. Sal's face didn't look any different, although several centimetres of luxuriant raven hair had now displaced the dyed stuff around her scalp, suggesting a two-tone cyber-goth effect. Sal had been in the Chronosphere for twelve months, about three months longer than Raffi, and a month longer than Dario, and the Moon Effect would have hit her proportionally harder than it had them. Anna had changed in ways other than hair length. According to Sal, Anna had been here for three and a half years and had been twenty-three when she entered. Even though she'd been living in reverse for most of that time, the Moon Effect clearly paid no heed to that. It aged you exactly as much as if you'd been living that period in the normal world and in the customary temporal direction. Having been nineteen just a minute ago, Anna was now in her mid-twenties. Raffi thought she actually looked closer to thirty, but that was probably because of the traumas she'd undergone.

There were three others in the room. The attendant was one of them. The impact for him had been physical – and fatal – the man's body had been smashed by the door as it had swung outwards.

Behind Raffi were two more prone figures. Fearing what he might find, he hobbled towards them. Where Jonah had once been, Raffi saw a frighteningly thin man in very late middle age, perhaps early sixties. His hair was a grey-brown storm that stood out from his head like a shout of distress. His shapeless white beard stuck out at every angle, like the last, desperate nest of a dying bird. Within it, Raffi saw his open pink mouth, breathing. Every bone in his face stood clear behind the smooth pale vellum of his skin. He'd seen this face before, just after his first meeting with Jonah. This was the real Jonah – a true reflection of his years, no longer masked by the cosmetic effects of a life lived at chronospheric speed. His brown eyes, open, were fixed on nothing that Raffi could see. He looked conscious, but in shock. His arm was outstretched, his hand clutching at the hand – if that was what it was – of the dead figure next to him.

Claw was perhaps a better term for it. The corpse, enveloped in outsized clothing, was long of limb, but made small by its hunched, foetal posture. Its skin, where observable, was like glossy brown shoe leather, stretched tight over thin, yet horridly visible bones. A few wisps of grey-blonde hair clung like tenacious weeds to the fragile brown dome of the scalp. The face was a shrunken balloon of dense furrows and wrinkles, the eyes clamped shut within cavernous sockets. The collapsed nose sloped towards a lipless mouth of teeth in a rictus smile of agony. Something in the shape of the cheekbones that now poked sharply through the shrivelled skin spoke to Raffi of the Lastara he had once known. He recalled the first time he ever saw her, asleep on Jonah's bed. He remembered thinking she had the most perfect face he'd ever seen. Then, later, while she was kissing him, he'd glimpsed for the briefest moment her true appearance – identical to the face before him now.

He heard Dario crawl over to join him. 'She told me she was one of the first to enter the Chronosphere,' Raffi whispered. 'Avon Drak brought her here, while she was still numb with grief from the loss of her father. She's spent the past 100 odd years trying and failing to come to terms with that loss. I thought maybe there was a chance for her now with Jonah. Sadly it wasn't to be.'

'It's probably for the best,' said Dario. 'She's not suffering any more. But Jonah – Jonah's going to suffer alright, once he's returned to his senses.' They both looked at him. He was breathing and blinking, but his eyes were empty. 'Looks like he may have taken permanent leave of them, poor bloke.'

'He was lying about doing the hyperdilation, wasn't he?' said Raffi.

'Of course he was. He knew it would have killed Lastara and done this to him.'

'So then what was his plan? This would have happened to them anyway when the Chronosphere docked in six months time, only more slowly and painfully.'

'It was never going to dock,' said Sal.

Raffi and Dario looked at her in surprise. She was now sitting up, cradling her sister's head in her lap.

'Hey!' Dario cried. 'Thank Bo you're okay!'

'If a little bigger than I expected,' Sal smiled sadly.

'What do you mean it was never going to dock?' said Raffi.

'The Drakites were never going to let Carinae expose them to external justice,' said Sal. 'This temporal breach has to be their work. They were probably hoping to kill Carinae by instigating a Moon Effect throughout the Sphere. Once in control, they would have decelerated away from normal time. But they failed by the looks of it.' She pointed at something near the floor behind them. Raffi turned to see that the tiny entrance to the lobby had been replaced by a black and yellow striped metal screen. 'Someone acted quickly to seal off the Chronosphere from external time. Carinae is safe for now. But I'm sure they'll try again. My guess is that the Chronosphere will always be out there, drifting in time. It'll never come home. Jonah knew that.'

Raffi limped over to the strip of windows that ran across the top of the lobby's rear wall, which were now at head height. He looked out at the Chronosphere interior. It was like a model, with tiny yellow segments of park and lines of wrecked buildings even now in the process of being demolished by toy-sized bulldozers and cranes with wrecking balls. Time Tower looked no more than ten metres high. No wonder this place wasn't visible from the outside. Of course! It all made sense now. They must have been miniaturised in the temp-al chambers before they entered. That was the technological leap Carinae's scientists had made. The Chronomaster had talked about how they'd developed a revolutionary new means of shielding the body from superfast speeds, not by using suits, but by altering the body itself. That revolutionary new means was miniaturisation. They made people smaller. Tiny things are much better at moving fast. One only had to look at the way insects buzz around to see that.

'So what now?' asked Dario. Are we trapped in here?'

'No, of course not,' said Sal. 'We can leave any time we like.' She pointed to the far end of the room. Through a veil of dust and smoke they saw enormous cracks in the wall surrounding the tiny temp-al chamber door. Through the cracks shone the unmistakable gleamings of daylight. 'We're in real time now,' Sal reminded him, 'and through there lies the real world.'

The Language of the Chronosphere

air tennis Similar to conventional tennis, except players wear hoverjet heels and the net is six metres high.

Celestial Sphere An idealised future Chronosphere, permanently separated from the outside world, in which human beings are able to discover their true potential, becoming better, brighter, stronger and more virtuous.

chrono-dome A dome-shaped device used for treating wounds. The chrono-dome works by compressing time, like a miniature Chronosphere, so that it can heal wounds quickly.

Chronomaster The ruler of the Chronosphere.

chrono-san A low-ranking security officer in the Chronosphere.

chrono-sensei The highest-ranking official in the Chronosphere, below Chronomaster.

Chronosphere Short for 'Hyperbaric Chronosphere' – a sphere in which time is compressed, so that its inhabitants can experience an entire year in the space of a single real-world minute.

cognitive inference deception (CID) A mask of light pixels worn for the purpose of disguise. The pixels are so arranged that, when perceived by an observer, they collectively form an unresolved picture of a face that must then be interpreted by the brain according to its particular expectations. People who already know the person beneath the mask will see him or her as they are, but strangers will see only an anonymous human face.

coolfizz A cool, fizzy drink which comes in auto-cooled cans. You choose the flavour you want by pressing the desired button on the can.

darkness generator A photon-blocking device that can create a three-dimensional area of darkness for the purpose of concealing a person or object.

desynchronisation A process that shifts an individual's temporal perception backwards or forwards, so that their experience of the present occurs before or after other people's.

dilate In the Chronosphere, to dilate someone is to to everyone else, they appear to slow down (and, for the dilated person, the world around them appears to speed up).

dilator Short for 'anabaric dilator' – a gun that dilates its victims, making them appear to slow down or freeze.

domicile (dom) An apartment.

Drakites Followers of Avon Drak.

eathouse A restaurant.

gallium nitride Most artificial lighting in the 22nd century is by gallium nitride diode, which emits brilliant light at very little cost.

Garden The Garden is an idyllic place at the very bottom of the Chronosphere. It is the home of the Seed Race.

glitterstring A guitar with a single multi-note and vari-tonal string.

holoflick A hologrammatic, three-dimensional movie.

holographic replicon A replica of a person, made of light. The most sophisticated replicons can move, talk and behave almost exactly like their originals.

holoplex A public theatre showing holoflicks.

hoverbike A vehicle ridden in the style of a 20th- and 21st-century motorcycle, except it doesn't have wheels and it flies. It is propelled by an electrohydrodynamic thruster, powered by a nanowire battery or solid oxide fuel cell.

hypercap time Time spent in the hyper-dilatory chrono-capsule for purposes of restoring spatio-temporal equilibrium. The longer a person spends in the

Chronosphere, the more hypercap time he or she must do upon leaving.

hyper-dilatory chrono-capsule A device used by ex-Chrononauts. The 'hypercap' restores spatio-temporal equilibrium to a person's mind and body following a visit to the Chronosphere. Inside the Chronosphere, residents occupy time more densely than space; inside the hypercap, they experience the opposite. Days of hypercap time feel like seconds to the person in the capsule. Ex-chrononauts can either restore their spatio-temporal equilibrium in easy, convenient stages in a hypercap, or else nature will eventually rip it from them, violently and suddenly, when they least expect it. The latter is known as the Moon Effect, and it can be very unpleasant, even lethal.

invitro-sausage / invitroburger Synthetic meat grown in bioreactors.

Island City Short for 'Channel Island City', the large, artificial island in the English Channel. Home to Londaris's super-rich elite and the location of the Time Store and the Chronosphere.

levitator A transparent tube that conveys human passengers, usually in a vertical direction, by means of magnetic levitation.

light disc The illuminated disc upon which levitator passengers stand as they are whisked upwards or downwards.

Londaris A vast metrostate occupying south-eastern England and north-western France.

MAID A Multitasking, Autonomous, Interactive Device. MAIDs are computers equipped with friendly personalities. They provide a complete range of domestic services, including washing, dressing, cooking and cleaning, as well as expert advice and opinions, customised to the individual tastes of their master or mistress.

menial A small robot employed by a MAID to carry out a particular domestic task.

Moon Effect The physical law that states that subjective time has elastic qualities, and that if you stretch it, it will want to squeeze back on itself like an elastic band. People aren't generally aware of it because in their day-to-day lives time only gets stretched or compressed by tiny amounts. But the serious time-compression that takes place in the Chronosphere creates a very noticeable Moon Effect. The law is named after Prometheus Moon, the man who first noticed it.

outlands The poorer suburbs of the Londaris metrostate.

paradisiac A pill that intensifies a person's enjoyment of an experience. There are paradisiacs available for most areas of human experience, including music, love and food. Critics point out that people who take paradisiacs lose the ability to enjoy an experience directly, without artificial enhancement.

Paridex Short for the Paridex Annual Under-18 Hoverbike Championships – a yearly tournament held at the Paridex Municipal Hover Track in North-Central Londaris.

Punishment and Experimentation Centre (PEC) A hexagonal room in the Underside of the Chronosphere in which misbehaving prisoners suffer innovative time tortures.

Re-Education (Re-Ed) Centre A large subterranean gulag in the Underside of the Chronosphere where inmates are desynchronised and placed in 'time-locked' cells.

resynchronisation A process that restores a desynchronised person's temporal perception so that their experience of the present corresponds with everyone else's.

rezzy flash A symptom of a botched resynchronisation, in which the victim periodically experiences brief flashes of the past or future.

saporiac A paradisiac that improves the flavour of food.

Secrocon The organisation that runs the Chronosphere.

Seed Race An elite group of specially selected teenagers whose task is to begin the process of building a new and better world within the Chronosphere.

sensovision An entertainment and information medium in which three-dimensional moving images float in front of the viewer's eyes.

temp fi-er Short for 'temporal field eraser' – a gun that can erase a person's temporal field, deleting them in time as well as space. A temp fi-er doesn't just kill a person, it changes the past so that the person was never born.

temp-al chamber A chamber through which a person enters the Chronosphere.

temp-al duct A passage through which food and other supplies are sent into the Chronosphere.

temporal field An energy field that determines an individual's perception of and relationship with time.

Time Store The organisation that owns the Chronosphere. The Time Store administers the Chronosphere in the outside world, while Secrocon runs it from within.

Time Tower The vast, hourglass-shaped edifice that dominates the skyline of the Chronosphere's Topside. The kilometre-high residential tower is located at the geometric centre of the Topside dome. Its ceiling blends with the ceiling of the Chronosphere.

time-locked cell A prison cell in the Re-Education Centre. Time-locked cells don't need walls as prisoners are separated from one another in time.

time-looped Sent in a looped pattern through time, so that one experiences the same moment again and again.

time-reversed Reversed in time, so that one experiences time in the opposite direction to everyone else.

time-shifted Another term for 'desynchronised' – shifted backwards or forwards in time.

Topside The Topside is the topmost part of the Chronosphere. It is a dome-shaped space of around six kilometres diameter and a kilometre in height at its apex. This is the public section of the Chronosphere, where visitors from the outside world spend their time.

transradial Any of the transparent, tube-shaped, mag-lev conveyors that transport passengers from Time Tower Terminus to the Topside perimeter.

Tricarno Subjective Time Dilator This forerunner of the Chronosphere was built in 2158 by three physicists, Slim Trifid, Edo Carinae and Puppis Nova. The Tricarno was itself a development of earlier theoretical work performed by Prometheus Moon in the 2140s.

u-doll The official currency of Londaris.

Underside The vast space in the Chronosphere that exists beneath the Topside.

virtuarium A black sphere of around two metres diameter that users enter to experience an alternate, computer-generated reality.

Vocational Training A two- to four-year period of training that all Londaris citizens undergo to prepare them for their chosen career.

wave riding A water sport in which riders surf on special 'waveboards' that float just above the water's surface. A wall of water vapour forms a hydrostatic barrier, retaining a cushion of compressed air beneath the board.

Zeno Space A dimension in which space and time are infinitely divisible, making it impossible to move from one place to another.

ACKNOWLEDGEMENTS

This book was partly inspired by the ideas contained in some classic science fiction stories, including H.G. Wells's 'The New Accelerator', Ian Watson's 'The Very Slow Time Machine' and Brian Aldiss's 'Man In His Time'.

I also consulted numerous fascinating and occasionally wacky websites to help me develop theories of time and create a plausible-seeming future. In particular, I would like to acknowledge Peter Lynds for his theories about Zeno's paradoxes, Michael Buchanan for his ideas about temporal fields, *The Observer*'s brilliant 'The Future of Food' feature, and Research Media and Cybernetics for the information on EHD thrusters, upon which the technology of the hoverbikes was loosely based.

On a personal note, I would like to thank my parents Emile and Anita, my sister Kelly, my brother-in-law Steven and my nephew Alistair for their helpful comments on earlier drafts of this book. I would also like to thank my sister Gabi for her support and her eagle eye, my brother Matthew for his enthusiasm, my editor Cath Senker for her helpful amendments, my 'first fan' Sue Greville Collins for her lovely comments and my eight-year-old son Michael for our inspiring conversations. Last but not least, I want to thank my wife Paola for her unwavering love and support.

ABOUT THE AUTHOR

Alex Woolf was born in Willesden Green, North London. He studied History and Politics at university.

He spent his 20s riding his motorbike, travelling and working, including a brief stint as a dish-washer in a roach-infested restaurant in Florida.

Since 2001, he has been an editor and author of children's books and has written on a wide range of subjects, from spiders to Nazis.

Alex lives in North London with his Italian wife and two children.

THE ADVENTURE CONTINUES...

CHRONOSPHERE

Book 3

Ex Tempora

by Alex Woolf

Life has not been easy for Raffi and his friends since their escape from the Chronosphere, but when they are drawn back to it on a rescue mission, they find a world very different from the one they had left.

The previous rulers have left a legacy of bitter conflict and religious fundamentalism, and it's up to Raffi and his time-altered companions to uncover the true motives of those who now wield power.

They'll encounter old friends and mechanised enemies on their journey. Sacrifices will be made and love lost and won, but will they be able to overcome the challenges and escape with their lives and minds intact?

COMING SOON

A division of Book House

CHRONOSPHERE

Book 3

Ex Tempora

PROLOGUE

avron Harker, Science Correspondent for Londaris Sensocast Corporation. Special Report: 2 March 2190: Six months have now passed since the incident on Blue Yonder Street that first drew worldwide attention to that phenomenon known as the Chronosphere. Since that time, the offices of the Time Store, the corporation responsible, have remained closed, pending the results of an investigation by the Justice Department. I can report that this investigation is not going well. Following the explosion that destroyed one of the access points to the Chronosphere on 2 September last year, all communications with the dome-shaped timeship have ceased. To the outside world, it seems dead. Yet some 10,000 people, most of them aged between 15 and 25, are believed to remain trapped within it, their fate unknown. When we first heard this figure of 10,000, most of us found it hard to accept. The Chronosphere is, after all, a dome of no more than 60 metres diameter. How could it possibly contain that quantity of people? But since those first bewildering weeks following the incident, the shadowy folk at the Time Store have been forced to come clean about some of their technology, which includes, apparently, a miniaturisation device for shrinking its inhabitants! Furthermore, we have learned that the Chronosphere is – as its name suggests – a sphere, not a dome, and the dome is no more than the visible tip of something much wider and deeper.

Breaking into the Chronosphere is, as we have discovered, out of the question, as it would immediately kill everyone inside, owing to the lethal consequences of the 'Moon Effect', which occurs when two different timespeeds collide. Extensive interviews with Time Store officials have yielded few clues about what could have happened on that September morning. Most agree that a limited Moon Effect event within the access chamber was probably responsible for the explosion, but how it happened and why communications immediately ceased thereafter, they cannot explain. They stress that the inner doors of the Chronosphere remain secure, and there is every reason to believe that it remains a functioning, life-sustaining environment for those on board.

Having drawn a blank at the Time Store, the investigators have attempted to communicate with the Chronosphere directly. Last December, a smaller version of the Chronosphere, known as the Minichron, was dispatched to intercept the stranded timeship. Just four metres in diameter, the Minichron was attached to the side of the larger sphere – its purpose: to seek out the Chronosphere wherever it currently resides in time. This was no longer merely a Justice Department investigation: it had become a rescue mission. The Minichron was our last, best hope of establishing a bridge to the Chronosphere, and bringing its young captives home... Well, we all know what happened next. The Chronosphere could not be found – anywhere. Christmas came and went without the longed-for gift of loved ones returning to their families. And then, after six fruitless weeks of searching, communications ceased with the Minichron. It, too, fell silent – and the four officials on board joined the ranks of all those other 'chrononauts', trapped in another time.

So, where did that leave the investigation? Well, following the Minichron debacle, officials pinned their hopes on eye-witness reports of a group of five individuals seen leaving through the ruined access chamber doors minutes after the explosion. The so-called 'Temp-Al Five' included two bearded young men, one of whom apparently only has one leg; two young women; and a man in his 60s bearing the corpse of an old woman. In late January, they managed to track down the older man – a fellow by the name of Jonah Grey. What do we know about Mr Grey? He was born in November 2172, making him, despite appearances, just 17 years old. He was found living in Camberley with his parents, both biomedical engineers in their 40s. Four weeks ago, while helping the Justice Department with its enquiries, Jonah Grey disappeared. His family and friends have no idea where he is. Some of them have publicly accused the Justice Department of abducting him – or worse – and the case has become something of an embarrassment to the government.

So here we are, six months on, no closer to uncovering the mystery of the Chronosphere or figuring out how to get its thousands of imprisoned inhabitants back home. The Justice Department continues its search for the Temp-Al Five while fending off allegations of a cover-up with regard to the missing man, Jonah Grey. Meanwhile, the families of the 10,000 have set up a permanent vigil outside the Time Store offices in Blue Yonder Street, waiting, watching, hoping…